WHERE *DO* THEY ALL COME FROM?

WHERE *DO* THEY ALL COME FROM?

a short story collection

Patty Friedmann

SARTORIS
LITERARY
GROUP

A traditional publisher with a non-traditional approach to publishing

For Esme and Werner,
The best characters I ever dreamed up

Beatles' Prescience Reflected in Government Action

LONDON (International News Service)—It took over half a century, but the British government has acted on a serious problem that the iconic Beatles put to music back in 1966.

"I know it was my cousin Eleanor they sang about in that song about all the lonely people," said George Rigby, 87. "It took this long for the government to address the problem."

Today Prime Minister Theresa May appointed a Minister of Loneliness.

"I expect a lot of flowers for Cousin Eleanor at St. Peter's Church graveyard in Liverpool now that there's no more stigma attached to being lonely," said Rigby. "I wish Father M had lived to see this day."

Copyright © 2018 Patricia Friedmann
Cover Photo Credit: Caren Nowak
Library of Congress Control Number: 2018933889
ISBN: 978-0-9913745-8-8

Sartoris Literary Group, Inc.
Jackson, Mississippi
www.sartorisliterary.com

CONTENTS

WHERE *DO* THEY ALL COME FROM?

ASHES, ASHES

Wilson and Zib are flying up to meet me, and Woodrow is in a mahogany box on the front seat. I couldn't stand the idea of walking into Arlington Cemetery with Woodrow in a cardboard carton, so I took him back to Lamana-Panno-Fallo last week and had him transferred.

They were discreet, taking him into the back where I didn't have to see, like he was in his underwear in a dressing room in a department store; if I wanted to watch, I only had to ask. I'm curious about most things, but I could live forever without seeing Woodrow look like something at the bottom of a barbeque pit.

Arlington is overcrowded; they won't let you in unless

you're cremated or famous. Woodrow was in the Marines; his mama never fed him, let him pick collard greens off the neutral ground like a colored boy; it was the military or jail. He never got past Subic Bay and crab lice, but he saw the Kennedy funeral on TV in 1963 and that settled it for him. He's not getting a horse with backwards stirrups or anything, but they told me they'd get three guys out there to shoot off seven rounds. Or seven guys to shoot off three. I didn't write it down.

I stay at the Bulldog Inn just past Atlanta. Everything flushes, flows, and blows when it's supposed to, and I don't see any reason to look for anything fancier. I'm somewhere in between Woodrow and Zib when it comes to motels. Woodrow figured you could reach any point in the continental United States with only one motel stop: drive twenty-four hours, stop twenty-two hours, check-in to check-out, get your money's worth, drive twenty-four more, get to Maine or Washington State for forty dollars plus food and gas. Zib wants to stop in city hotels, tour and swim and spend. Zib will not go more than two hundred miles by car, then she has to take a plane.

"Suit yourself," she says, "but I am not going to act like a poor person."

This from someone who lives like a nun, one room, no furniture to speak of. She never goes to the doctor. Zib puts all her money in clothes and throwaways, wears disposable contact lenses, works as an assistant manager at the Winn-

Dixie someplace in Florida, used to hit Woodrow for five dollars whenever she saw him. She's like these colored people in my neighborhood. They live in about six hundred square feet, roof leaking, no air conditioning, but they drive up and down in top-of-the-line Buicks.

I don't understand a thing about Wilson. Wilson goes wherever and however anybody tells him to: he gets a wife who wants to stay in the Plaza in New York, so he stays in the Plaza in New York, he gets a grant that puts him in a lean-to in darkest Africa, so he sits for three months in a lean-to in darkest Africa. He teaches Organic Evolution, says we're all going to be psychics one day. I don't know why I surround myself with people who are so extreme.

***

The last time Woodrow and I drove this route, it was two-lane undivided highways, and I had two children who pounded each other senseless in the back seat. We took both cars because Woodrow said we couldn't agree on what we were supposed to be doing on a vacation. I wanted to go see my great aunt in Richmond, Virginia, since there was a good chance she might leave me something one day, but Woodrow thought that a vacation meant going to a battlefield and standing by a termite-infested cannon and pretending you could see men blowing holes in each other across what was now nicely mown grass. I think Woodrow didn't want to fight me over the cigarette smoke. I took Wilson and Zib in the car with me because Woodrow wouldn't know what to do with them, and I made it as far as Atlanta before I told him to pick one, either one, or I'd kill both of them. Naturally he picked Zib, which made me happy, because, even though she was the girl, she was the heller of the two, and you could count on Wilson to sit in the front seat with a Big Chief tablet and write down all the states he saw license plates from.

Trouble was, halfway across South Carolina, I got a flat tire. I was following Woodrow, because, all else aside, Woodrow could read a map, and I'd rather not. I slowed up, started to pull over to the shoulder, realized he was no more paying attention to me than he ever had; he was going to get all the way into North Carolina before he noticed I wasn't behind him. So I went tearing behind him, blasting the horn, riding on the rim, sixty miles an hour, and Wilson was screaming, "Mama, no, Mama, no," and I leaned on the horn, but Woodrow never looked in the rearview mirror.

I couldn't see Zib, who'd flapped around in the motel pool the night before until she was so crazy about herself that she couldn't sleep. I pushed the accelerator to seventy, and the car was rocketing along like it was going to explode, and right after we came out of a curve I pulled into the other lane until I was riding next to him, and I stayed there until he looked over to see who the fool was, playing chicken on a two-lane undivided highway. We had to get a tow truck, the wheel was so messed up. Turned out he was listening to a boxing match on the radio.

While the car was in the shop, we checked into a motor

court, expecting to stay two nights, and Woodrow was beside himself over the unplanned expense. "We're halfway north, what're these people doing with air conditioning?" he said, like it was costing us extra. Woodrow worked security at the Whitney Bank vault in New Orleans, so all he heard all day were the sounds of downtown air conditioning and boxes full of valuables, and he came home nights beat and fussy and turned off our only unit and watched "Hogan's Heroes" like Hogan was some kind of military genius.

Woodrow only closed the windows in December, January, and February, like there weren't any colored boys fearless enough to climb into a person's house and leave him for dead. He paid off the mortgage in ten years with what he saved on NOPSI, never mind that he could have gotten himself a Schedule A and had enough leftover every year that I could have bought my underwear someplace besides Krauss's.

"We take one car up to Virginia, we come back for yours on the way home," he said. "Save on gas, too."

I told him I'd consider his plan, though I didn't plan to go all the way across North Carolina and most of Virginia without a cigarette. We'd be in his car, his rules, and he didn't like the smell of smoke, even though he didn't mind the smell of mildew from the time Zib left the windows open in a rainstorm. I figured something would come up. All that ever got me my way with Woodrow was dumb luck.

That night Zib woke up moaning that she was going to

throw up. All of us in that one room, Woodrow snoring like a fool, Wilson with his fists balled up around his face like he was going to block out something, naturally I was the only one going to hear Zib.

"Serves you right," I said, not opening my eyes, trying to stay asleep. She had put away five burgers from White Castle. Five minutes later, she was over the toilet, three feet from my bed, barfing her guts up.

"Serves you right," she said when I jumped out of bed.

Zib, who had said she wanted to eat in a restaurant where they starched the napkins, said to Woodrow, "You all act like we're poor. This is too embarrassing for words."

I pulled her outside the cabin, and her big yellow Jackie Kennedy walleyes got wide. At home I smacked her for sass; in the yard I chased her with the garden hose, nozzle tight, because it wasn't any of the neighbors' business.

"Calm down, I just don't want you waking your brother with all that racket," I whispered.

Some valve in her must have shut to spite me, because the color came back in her face. I waited with my arms folded across my chest. The air filled with mosquitoes, and I slapped at them with no patience.

"I can't just throw up because you want me to," Zib said.

"Get some air," I told her, and we stood out there staring toward the highway. We had a sliver moon and clouds; I could see nothing beyond what light we were giving off ourselves. No cars were passing, only one other cabin was occupied, and I found myself wishing for a little traffic. The owner was an old talker, and I figured he needed to average four customers a night or he would have to die long before he looked like he was going to.

I thought about going in and getting a cigarette. I was straining for the sound of cars on the road, and Zib was rocking side to side like she was trying to put herself to sleep standing up. She let out a little yelp, like a puppy dog when you step on its tail. I clapped my hand over her mouth, and her lips were still wet with bile and thick spit. She tried to talk, and I pulled my hand away, sticky.

"Don't move," a man's voice said from behind me.

Naturally, I turned around. No man is going to talk to me like that. Especially in the middle of nowhere. I saw the gun before I saw his face. Woodrow. His service revolver pointed right at me. I broke up laughing. I'd always figured that if I needed an operation or something, the first thing I'd do was rob the Whitney Bank vault. Woodrow and that rusty old tinker toy couldn't scare anybody. His hand was shaking. I could see it, in the dark.

"It's illegal to have that, Pop," Wilson said, coming up from behind him.

"It's illegal to steal pens from the Whitney Bank, too, but your father has reasons," I said, working hard not to laugh.

"Shut up, Jerusha," Woodrow said, all insulted. "You wouldn't think it was so funny, some crazy guy out here in the bushes trying to rob us." He put his arm around Wilson's

17

shoulder, led him back into the cabin.

"I got a marksmanship medal in Korea," I heard him telling the child. And Wilson shook his head up and down like it mattered to him. Wilson was an odd boy from the start, the kind who'd have the nerve to ask why all the music I listened to had words. The way he let his sister pick at him, I was sure he was going to be a queer.

"Sorry," I hollered behind Woodrow. I don't know if he heard me.

As it turned out, my car was ready the next afternoon, and we pulled off while there was still five hours of daylight. When I got home I told the whole story to Gloretta up the block, and it got sad instead of funny.

"That man's proud of himself," Gloretta said.

***

Right now it would be nice to see that old blue Ford station wagon bucking down the interstate ahead of me, all the windows closed and everything. I'd still think Woodrow was foolish, but it'd be nice.

When you live in a city like New Orleans your entire life, and then you get out on the road, I guess it's natural to get careless. Or to dare fate. I don't feel like being a prisoner all the time, locking this and locking that, and when I go down the highway a few miles past Atlanta and find a McDonald's, I leave the windows open so I won't burn my backside when I come back. Here it is, late October, and a heat wave over the entire southern United States is moving east like it's chasing me. Woodrow picked out that car, and we didn't figure out why we got such a bargain until the first time we tried to sit on black vinyl seats. Ronnie Lamarque must've gotten one car with black interior and couldn't unload it on anybody else. Woodrow always told me to stop complaining, but then he never wore skirts.

Everything is in the trunk, except a road map, a brown paper bag with four apples left in it, and a yellow throw pillow from my living room sofa that I sometimes tuck behind me when I'm driving. And Woodrow. I put Woodrow and the apples down on the floor to get them out of the sun. I swear I've only been in McDonald's for ten minutes; how long can it take to put away a cold sweet roll and coffee that tastes like unpurified Mississippi River water. When I come out, the apples are there, but Woodrow is gone.

***

I run back in here, and I guess I look like a crazy woman, but I don't care. There are only about a dozen people in the whole place, and I stand where you line up to put in your order, and I scream. "My husband's gone. I left him on the floor of the car, and somebody took him."

The girl who sold me my coffee twenty minutes ago backs away from her register with the kind of look on her face she'd have if I was swinging an AK47 rifle around the place and asking for nothing except revenge. I always thought I liked going in for fast food in the boonies, because they hire these Amy Carter-looking girls who twang and smile, but I guess for my purposes, in an emergency it's better to get one of those moody colored women you find in New Orleans. At least in the city nothing surprises anybody.

"Look, you fool, I don't mean my real husband," I say to the girl. "I mean my husband's ashes. He's in a box, and the box is gone."

She has a smile on the bottom half of her face. I'm crying, and I don't like to cry even in private. I tell her to get me the manager, and she scoots off, relieved like I've told her she can have the week off with pay.

Even the managers in these places are white and about nineteen years old. "Oh, Jesus," I say when I see him. "What good are you going to be?"

"Ma'am?" he says, and I have to start all over.

"My husband died. I had him cremated. I'm taking him up to Arlington. National Cemetery. Outside Washington. In a box. Okay?"

He nods, and I can tell he wishes he'd gone into watch repair or something else instead.

"So I come in here to eat. I eat. I go back to the car. And the box isn't there!"

"Oh, God," he says. Probably he's never known a dead person before. And McDonald's is not where you expect to find dead people. They go off somewhere else to die, like mice who eat rat poison.

"Call 911," he says to my cashier, who's standing behind the display case that is full of salads at eight-thirty in the morning.

I am tempted to tell him, No, don't do that. For all I know, transporting Woodrow across state lines is a federal offense. Though how else I'm supposed to get him up there is beyond me. I can see me telling my grandchildren, Oh, Grandpa Woodrow got lost in the mail. Wilson isn't the sort to raise children with any sort of sense of humor. And Zib isn't the sort to raise children at all.

Though the idea of saying, Oh, Grandpa Woodrow got stolen in a parking lot of the McDonald's someplace outside East Jesus, Georgia, is not a lot better. Not to mention how Woodrow himself is feeling about this now. I've known ever since I married him that Woodrow was going to come back and haunt me if he died first. Even if he died in his sleep. From what I see on "Unsolved Mysteries," the only people who come back as ghosts are the ones who were murdered or killed themselves. I figure that has to do with having unfinished business, and all his life Woodrow had unfinished business. Really, he had unstarted business. Woodrow needs to be in Arlington Cemetery.

The manager has given me a cup of coffee, and I sit in this booth for a few minutes trying to decide if I'm going to drink it to be polite. I'm thinking in my head, in case Woodrow can hear me, Look, Woodrow, I am terribly sorry. I could've brought you inside, but I didn't want people sitting in here to see me hugging this box, acting like I'm some lunatic or like I've got a million dollars in unmarked bills inside.

Not that Woodrow would say anything. He was the kind who stewed. Very quietly, and it sometimes took a year to figure out that I'd done something that got on his nerves. And then only if I did it again.

"Remember last July when you let the brake tag expire? Once is stupid, Jerusha, twice is damn stupid. What you pay in penalty'd buy a bag of groceries."

A bag of groceries to Woodrow was the international standard of currency, though I don't know how, since he had the idea that nothing had changed since 1939, which is about when he bought his last bag of groceries. Anyway, I don't know how spirits let you know they're stewing, but I imagine they have their ways, and I don't want to spend the next year being jumpy about going into rooms by myself.

It takes the police over an hour to come. It's breaking into my driving time, but I can't leave and cut my losses since the whole point of going up there is to have Woodrow with me. The manager brings me another cup of coffee, and I line it up next to the first one, which is still full. I don't think he realizes that I'm on my way somewhere, and the last thing I need is to be so full of coffee that I shake and pee all the way down the road. I light up a cigarette, dare anyone to say anything. Both my children sent me this article from the *Wall Street Journal* about secondhand smoke, like I couldn't figure out they were blaming me for killing their father.

Two officers walk in, and they both order a sausage biscuit and a Coke before they come sit down at the table with me. "How much you pay for the box?" one asks me when I've told him the whole story. "See, I'm not sure what kind of crime this is exactly."

"The box cost me $79.95 plus tax, but the stuff inside the box cost me fifty years of pure aggravation," I say. The second one looks at me like I'm using big words. "That's my husband in that box. Human remains. Grave robbing. Whatever you want to call it, it's not stealing a $79.95-plus-tax box."

They tell me to stay here. It's getting to the fringes of the lunch hour, and I can tell the manager is unnerved that I am still going to be sitting here when all his happy, hungry customers come in. He's at an interstate exit, for Chrissakes, you'd think he'd be used to everybody coming in on some level of adventure, then going away without remembering they've been here, but I can tell he wants me out of here, before I scare people off, sending a message up and down the highway that crazy old women are sitting in his restaurant telling stories about grave robbers. This is the first time in my life that I see myself as an old lady. Generally I figure I'm still a kid. After all, I can ride a bicycle and rollerskate.

The policemen come back in a few minutes. They look full of self-importance, and they beckon me out of the restaurant. I pick up my purse, and the manager smiles and waves goodbye. "I might be back," I say.

"Fine, fine," he says with that mushmouth accent of his. Fahn, fahn.

This little strip of feeder highway may look like it's nothing but one franchise after another, but there's a lot of pieces of red raw land lying around the parking lots, full of bulldozer and truck tracks. The policemen take me out into the McDonald's parking lot, and one says, "You think you could identify the remains?"

I tell him no, that I made a point of not seeing what Woodrow looked like burned to a crisp. "Just ashes, maybe five pounds of ashes," I say. I remember this article in *The Star* about this cut-rate crematorium in California that crammed fifteen bodies in one oven, smashed up the bones with a shotput, then shoveled ashes out of oil drums with coffee cans, three pounds for a woman, five pounds for a man.

They walk me past the parking lot droppings that you usually only see at Schwegmann's, a disposable diaper coming unwrapped and stinking in the sun, the dumpings from a car ashtray. I look at the ashtray mess, Doublemint gum wrapper, a couple of butts, some ashes that haven't blown away, and I hope that wasn't what Lamana-Panno-Fallo was sending up to Arlington.

"That's not him," I say to one officer.

"Didn't think so," he says seriously.

They walk me over to a construction area next to McDonald's, and I see what looks to me like a stomped ant pile in the middle of the red Georgia clay. It takes me a second to realize that ants use what's available, that ant piles take on

"Call 911," he says to my cashier, who's standing behind the display case that is full of salads at eight-thirty in the the color of the land, that the little mound of gray-black is probably Woodrow.

"Aw, shit," I say, not daring to get any closer.

"Think that's it?" the other officer says, and I nod.

They walk over to the Woodrow pile, and I stay where I am. They're used to dead people, but they move quietly, like they're going to disturb somebody sleeping with a gun tucked under him.

"Yeh, fresh footprints," I hear one say. Men get such a charge out of that detective game. They come back to me, tell me there's nothing more they can do.

I say, "What'm I supposed to do?" The idea of scooping up Woodrow myself makes me crazy. After all, every handful was one time some part of him that was full of nerves. One time when Wilson was no more than ten, we were at the dinner table, and he said, "Mama, you realize that if I were doing this while the chicken was alive it'd be screaming with pain?" He said, "You realize if someone took a bite this big out of you that they'd rush you into surgery and try to connect everything back again?" I told him to get away from the table and not to come back until he could stop the disgusting talk.

Wilson said, "Well, now I'm not particularly hungry anyway, and he refused to eat meat for about six months after that. I could see myself scooping up every part of Woodrow except a hand or a liver, only to get to Judgment Day and find him standing there without all his parts and refusing to talk to me.

I holler after the officers. "I'll pay you," I say.

"Ma'am?" one says. I could grow to hate that form of respect.

"I said, I'll pay you to help me get him back in my car." They look at each other, like boys shooting dares, and one says, "Aw, ma'am, no need to pay."

Half an hour later I am back on the road. Woodrow, and a few bits of Georgia clay, is lying inside a paper sack from McDonald's. I figure I'll get to the motel before the kids, mold the bag around until you can't see the red clumps anymore, and run out and buy a new wooden box. I can't leave Woodrow in a McDonald's bag. McDonald's is all into saving the earth, so this bag is not made to last an eternity. Besides, I wouldn't want to hear what Zib would say.

The story was originally published in *Short Story* and is used with permission.

LIANA

My first impression of Rolla was that he was a queer old man, a true asset in the neighborhood. It was after nightfall, and that made a difference: only extreme cues are given under streetlamps. His hair was gray, and had probably been graying for some time, for it had silver glints in it, though they didn't necessarily make him attractive. His body was cast from Balzac's mold: spindles of limbs, a paunch so grand it was practically regal. He was walking his dog by the cemetery. She had a coffee table back and arthritic bowlegs, and she doddered along, crapping at will.

The cemetery was an anonymous public place then. We

had just moved in across the street, and all the grassy spaces outside its fence seemed free for dropping dog turds and phlegm and go cups. Rolla seemed to be doing the perfectly civic thing, walking his dog there, instead of letting her go in someone's thick St. Augustine. Unlike the cemetery, the houses were inhabited by living people, who walked across their lawns and probably paid men with trucks full of broken-down lawnmowers a hundred dollars a month to keep each blade about an inch and a quarter long.

I hadn't met Alfred the cemetery caretaker yet, the man who had to clean up the messes Rolla was making. Alfred was a toothless black man who was actually older than Rolla by maybe fifteen years, as it turned out. But that night I didn't judge what Rolla was doing one way or the other. I just drew little pictures around him. He probably had grandchildren.

It was quarter to ten, a Friday night, and it seemed fine to let Sarie stay up late and go out with me in the dark for ice cream. We wouldn't have done that where we had lived before, a different part of the city where over and over we were told of the hazards. Most regular neighborhoods here lie between the streetcar route and bad-ass trashed up blocks where all the people who have to ride public transportation live. New Orleans is a city of facades, like Philadelphia or Chicago, where you can ride the standard famous streets, the same ones where the poor people travel underground or way up in the air, and think that it's a most exquisite place to live. But those poor people go sound blasting through those facades and keep on walking until they get to their rooms that stink of rotten onions and have a washing machine rigged up next to the toilet but no dryer.

We had been told about that at our old house so often. It was two blocks from the streetcar in one direction and six blocks from the river in the other. Those people walking toward the river were poorer the farther they had to go, and I imagined they got angrier and angrier the more they had to walk past the nice houses with the hand-planed lawns. We hadn't gone out at night there. But this was a new neighborhood, and we were alone now; I figured we'd learn as we went along.

We walked out the side door of the house, and there was Rolla, over by the cemetery, watching his dog as she squatted, not looking off in the distance the way I would have. Even in the dark I could tell that he thrilled to see us. He called out to Sarie as if he had known her for quite some time.

"Good evening," he said in the voice of Donald Duck. As clear as Donald Duck can be; I could understand what he was saying. Sarie was absolutely silent. "And how are you this evening?" he said, still an exact Donald Duck. I began to laugh, because that is what happens when a person is addressed in a Donald Duck voice; it is one of life's totally perfect experiences.

He just kept walking. I can look back at his doing that now and see that it made sense. Walking around the cemetery every night, he had known, of course, that our tiny

29

house had been for sale. Then he'd seen it sold and then he'd seen it dumped to overflowing with two fractions of lives' worth of stuff that didn't go together or quite fit. He knew where to find us again, though we were completely unremarkable. Sarie was logical about him, proprietary about him, as if he were another fine oddity that came with the neighborhood, like the cemetery.

"We'll have to hold our breath all the time we're at home now."

"Or touch blue."

"I want to show him to Daddy," she said, forgetting.

"Rats," Sarie said as Rolla kept on walking. She looked at me as if I'd failed her in some way.

"It's hard to meet people when it's dark; you don't get much definition of them," I said laconically. I was feeling that lack of intensity it's possible to have in the dark; surely Rolla had felt it, too, to seem so indifferent.

He was in reality quite cunning when it came to making connections. "I saw your dog walking toward St. Charles Avenue yesterday afternoon," the man's voice said on the phone around eleven-thirty, two nights later. Our dog had run off: not adjusting to the neighborhood, or perhaps adjusting too well, she found a weak spot in the fence, and there was no way to know how long she had been gone when we noticed she was missing. We posted signs on the phone poles on every block within a quarter mile of our house. Our

30

address and phone number were on the sign. We never did that sort of thing in our old neighborhood.

"She just looked like she knew where she was going, so I didn't bother to stop her," the man said.

I had been wakened from that first deep part of sleep, and I found what he was telling me fairly useless. Our dog was a fast traveler; even knowing she was headed toward the river was of no help. There were a lot of places she could be between our new house and the river. Her only consistent pattern was that she never doubled back. I thanked the man on the phone.

"Hey, this is Donald Duck, from the other night," he said. I began to laugh. "Sleep well," he said, in his Donald Duck voice. Then he hung up.

When I was driving back up our street the next evening at supper time, I saw Rolla in front of what I figured was his own house. I had just retrieved the dog from someone on Coliseum Street just past the Lafayette Number One Cemetery. An elitist cemetery, right across from Commander's, full of fine old Protestant, Garden District families. Not like ours, with a big fat plot for infants from the German Orphanage, visible from our kitchen window. The guard at the Lafayette Cemetery had been shooing our dog out for two days, the woman told me.

Rolla waved, and I pulled over to show him my catch. "Someone read her tags," I told him.

"My tag," he said, and he handed me his business card. Rolla Conn, it said, Printing Sales. He had hand-written on it, "wife Caroline (rhymes with fine), daughter Liana." As if he'd been sure for quite a while that he was going to give me his card. "Liana's about the size of yours there," he said, pointing at Sarie. "About nine, right?"

"Right," I said, as I wrestled with the dog to keep her from leaping through the glass, going for Rolla or freedom, I couldn't tell which. She was harmless, just difficult and scrappy, a beautiful black lab with the spirit of a street dog; she could probably have survived indefinitely if I'd just been kind enough to let her go.

I pushed Sarie to call Liana. I supposed I could call Caroline, because that would be the natural thing to do, but I often functioned through Sarie, and she was too little to know how easy she was making things for me some of the time.

Sarie had to memorize the name, a spelling literalist with no auditory sense. Rhymes with Guiana, sort of. But that's not something Sarie could relate to. She just had to say it over and over again. "Can I talk to Liana?" A pause. "This is Sarie, can you come over?" The arrogance of childhood seemed exquisite to me sometimes.

Rolla delivered her to our door. By then I had seen Rolla twice, but at his age it was hard to tell what his child might look like. Age takes color away, not just hair pigment, but skin tones, and even sometimes eye color seems to lose its luminous quality if there ever was any. I had assumed that Rolla had children fully grown.

I opened the door. There, standing in the shadow of Rolla's considerable bulk, was a slip of an exquisite child. She had none of the darkness of the name Liana, but rather had pale gray eyes and light hair, hanging quite simply down past her shoulders. She had the bone structure of an Indian, but it seemed that was perhaps because she was so thin: high cheek bones, a full mouth. I suddenly pictured Rolla as having once been blond, though he had dark hazel eyes and a fine beak of a nose, and not very much chin. Liana's clothes seemed not quite right for her, a cheap dead-purple sweatsuit with a Care Bear at the left breast, the pants highwaters.

Rolla gently pushed her through the door, and she shambled off, as if she always found her way. "You heard the riddle about what's yellow and sleeps six?" Rolla asked.

"I give." We were standing on opposite sides of our threshold, and it would have been right to invite him in, his having sighted our lost dog. But I had too much to do.

"A Sewerage and Water Board truck!" he squealed. I laughed. Good joke, the kind that seems to pass from table to table in all those restaurants downtown where the men in seersucker eat their sandwiches at lunchtime and wangle big business deals over a $3.95 ham and swiss. Rolla didn't look the downtown type. When I'd seen him in front of his house he was decked out in pistachio polyester, down to his socks.

33

Today he was wearing a flaming red sports jacket and turquoise pants.

"You've got to get their attention when you're in sales," he said, waving his hand from the bow tie down past his equator. But it was Saturday.

"I'll ring the bell for her at six," he said. When I had fed her supper and seven-thirty had come and gone, I decided to return her to Rolla. I didn't mind Liana being there. She was a good laugher; she gave good audience to the bits of slapstick showing off that Sarie did. Sarie sucked a strand of spaghetti into her mouth, leaving bright orange minstrel lips. Liana laughed indulgently. Sarie tossed the dog a pinwheel cookie. "She'll still run away," she said, and Liana laughed again.

Rolla's business card was stuck up on the refrigerator. I could have phoned, but instead I chose to walk Liana back to her house. We began walking along in silence; Liana did not look like the type who enjoyed small talk though she was probably quite good at it. "I'm not afraid of the dark," she said quietly. "A lady was strangled to death in that house before we moved here." She pointed across the street. When we reached her house, she pounded on the front door, though there was a doorbell. I liked that, because I didn't think I could stand a child of the sort of delicacy that she appeared to have.

A woman answered the door. She was one of those women whose age is difficult to guess, especially when I was in my late thirties and having a hard time gauging my own exact age. She had short, very dark hair with a strand or two of silver, and pale gray eyes just like Liana's, but what I noticed first was that she had absolutely perfect white teeth. All the rest of her was generic, not tall or short, not fat or thin, not memorable at all. Even her clothes were forgettable, a simple cotton shirt and wrap skirt in a different color. She had on white-strapped sandals, the kind they sell every year in discount shoe stores, no matter what the current fashion.

Seeing Liana, she introduced herself and invited me in, effectively taking away whatever control there might have been in delivering the child and trying to get the evening over with. "You must come in." She spoke the way a decent sort of person might speak to a mental defective. Or a newly rich person might speak to a menial.

The house was strange in its lack of definition. They lived in half of a two-story Victorian double, painted a spirited yellow and dripping with gingerbread trim. That sort of house was costly to buy or rent because history was trendy, and in most houses like that the furniture showed striving to be in the current mode. In the living room there was little more than an early American settee—its upholstery had orange sailing ships and the Liberty Bell in green and cupolaed town halls in cream-color—and a well-worn braid rug. But the true oddity of the room was the curtains, made from a child's bed sheets, one with Strawberry Shortcake, another with Raggedy Ann and Andy. They'd been washed to fading, but not enough. There was no need for curtains;

35

nothing could go on in that room. Caroline waved her hand around the room, almost accusatory for the judgments she assumed I was making.

"I had surgery this winter right after we moved in. No time for curtains," she said, then kept going toward the back of the house with me following behind.

We passed through a dining room of more promise. The table was a mahogany oval with matching chairs. Nothing I would have chosen, because matching to me smacks of lack of thought, unless, of course, that thinking was done a century or so in the past. The table filled the room, so that no one could lean back in a chair more than about six inches. There was nothing else in the room except a sideboard, which was strewn with a child's drawings and windowed envelopes, some half-burned-down candles, and two serving bowls. The chair at that end of the room, I noticed, was crammed in so tightly between the sideboard and the table that no one could have sat in it. On the floor lay the coffee table-backed dog on a brown-stained blanket.

"She's sixteen, ought to be dead by now," said Caroline. "I swear she exists only to outlive me."

The back of the house, where Caroline was bringing me, was probably planned as a kitchen with a spacious breakfast nook. But the kitchen was in disarray that would take more than a single meal to create: a skillet half full of gray, hashed up food, dirty dishes with utensils actually stuck to them, a week's worth of newspapers. It seemed greasy back there,

36

more than anything. But she said, "Tea?" with the voice of a woman who would now ring for the butler, and I accepted.

"You probably don't work," she said, as she removed the skillet to a teetering pile of dishes in order to make room on the stove for the kettle. What she said lay somewhere between a question and an observation. A curious start.

"Why not?"

"I don't know. You look sort of unchallenged."

"All the more reason to work," I said. She didn't smile the way women who are friends with other women are supposed to.

"*What* do you do?"

"Research. Market analysis. Real estate."

We were already in an adversary confrontation, I could feel it.

"Slidell's the place to develop now," she said.

It seemed possible to just let her say that and find a way to go home. Slidell was not the place to develop now. Slidell was overbuilt and plastic.

"What looks like a boom to everybody else looks like a bust to us," I said.

"Perhaps you should reassess your data," she said.

"Do you have a vested interest in my doing so?" I said. A woman who made curtains out of a child's sheets, and foolish sheets at that, did not have the resources to be buying land in Slidell.

"Just your own credibility," she said as sweetly as if what she was saying was sweet itself.

I looked around the room, trying to think of something to comment on, some way to change the direction of our conversation. If the room had any coherence to it at all, it was in ducks. Duck magnets on the refrigerator, a print of a Michael Bedard duck, a Donald Duck mask, probably from Disney World. Rolla was too good to be sharing this space with her.

Caroline slammed the heel of her fist against the handle over the spigot on the sink. "God, he's useless," she said, as if contradicting me even in thought. "This damn sink has been broken for weeks. I'm going to do it myself, I swear."

"Are you okay now?" I asked, remembering she had mentioned surgery. An ambiguous question; see what she says.

"What?"

"You had surgery. Are you okay now?"

"I'm certain I must be. My doctor knew what he was doing." She ran her hand over the right side of her chest. It looked the same as the left one, but the gesture was too clear.

"Who's your doctor?"

"Dr. Shaskan."

"Oh, God," I said before I could think. Andy Shaskan was my high school classmate, whose performance back then was dangerously undistinguished. I remembered little of him, except a dazzling naivete. Shelley's "Indian Serenade" was the world's finest piece of poetry, he had argued, long after the teacher had called our bluff on it. Tripe, she had said, and he had held forth on its drama for a painful ten minutes. He had had a hard-on; I'd seen it. Certainly quite a number of brilliant diagnosticians have never understood literature, but I would not want one to treat me. And I would not let Andy Shaskan cut a sliver out of my finger. He might enjoy it too much.

Caroline looked at me queerly. "He and I went to school together," I said. "You know how those things go."

"No."

"How can you trust a man who jumped into the hotel pool fully clothed the night of graduation?" I gave her a little smile, but she didn't smile back.

"One minute," she said. The kettle still had not boiled. She went to the foot of the stairs and clapped her hands loudly, a dour old schoolmistress rounding up the stragglers on the playground. Nothing happened, and she clapped again, this time calling out Liana's name. Liana and Sarie had very quietly vanished when we walked in, and they had not made a noise that I could hear since. Liana came trudging down the stairs, her little sticks of legs making a minor drama of the effort, putting an extra bit of shuffle-kick into each step down.

"I don't hear you practicing," Caroline said.

"Okay," said Liana, who turned in her path and started up the steps again, saving herself that last bit of the descent

39

and return trip.

"And don't forget to say thank you to Sarie's mother," she said, as sweet as when she claimed to be protecting my credibility in wiping out weeks of my research in the breadth of a single idea of her own.

"Thank you," Liana said, and she sounded as if she meant it.

I was seduced by the way Caroline served us tea. She had a tea for every quirk, every malady. And an encyclopedic store of wrong facts on the value of each. I found myself drawn at first to ask for orange pekoe, just because I figured there was no comment a person could make on orange pekoe. But Caroline marched out all the rest, the Constant Comment, the Red Zinger, the English Breakfast, the Lapsang Souchong, all jumbled up in their bags, strings entwined, in a dust-streaked canister. I figured that after a while they would all taste the same, drawing on the aromas of one another, but my tea tasted just like what I might get in a greasy spoon downtown. Caroline used tap water, slamming more good-naturedly at the spigot this time.

"We use tap water," she said.

"You're fatalistic, I guess," I said. Tap water in New Orleans carries all the carcinogenic effluence of a thousand miles of dumping into the Mississippi.

"No," she said, as if I had called her the worst name possible. "I did a little experiment. I watered two plants, one with tap, one with spring. The tap water plant almost took

40

over the room inside of a week; the other one was sickly and shriveled. It died by the time it was six inches tall."

"I'm sure carcinogens make terrific fertilizer," I said.

She actually smiled, and I wanted to leave.

"I have sugar, honey, artificial sweetener. Lemon, cream, milk?"

"Milk and sugar," I said.

"One spoonful or two?"

"Make it three."

She served me my tea, she offered me English biscuits and nut cakes, cream cheese and pepper jelly and crackers. It was impulse food, late in the evening, eaten from nerves. But Caroline was putting a surfeit of pleasure in front of me. I took bits of textures, breaking off pieces, not counting. Caroline didn't talk much, just did little fragments of explaining. Sort of reading my mind, as she had done with the curtains.

"Rolla's been practicing Donald Duck since he was eight; his mother put him in boarding school, and I guess that's the way she managed," she said, her eyes scanning the room for a beginning point. Her gaze had rested on the Michael Bedard print of the duck in front of the bullet-riddled wall. Caroline shrugged, as if she had spent enough time somewhere along the line considering her mother-in-law.

I said nothing, testing. And steering clear of her contradictions. One thing I could already say about Caroline: she was an extreme sort of person, and extreme people are

41

easier to cope with. You just have to go to lazy extremes yourself; they never notice.

"Unless we buy the whole house, I don't see any reason to fix it up," she said.

"You don't own the house?" This seemed like an owner-occupied neighborhood, as my demographics might report. But in a double, someone's got to be renting.

"No, still settling up Rolla's first wife's estate. It's taken two years. We'll buy when it's settled."

"Two years? Liana's nine."

"And Liana's *mine*," she said. She sounded insulted.

Rolla came barreling in the back door a moment later, carrying a shopping bag from Harry's Hardware and looking most pleased with himself. "This ought to do it," he said, holding out the bag to Caroline. She looked at him skeptically, knowing right off that she'd surely catch him out.

Caroline glanced down into the bag, then looked up with great self-satisfaction. "It's not a Peerless. I told you *Peerless*. Take the goddamn thing back." She looked at me for sympathy, but I just looked at her. I turned to Rolla. He shrugged. "Harry's is closed. I'll have to go tomorrow," he said. Caroline rolled her eyes toward the ceiling, not caring if I saw Rolla her way or not.

I left all full of nut cakes and cream cheese and sweet tea, and I had the sort of exuberance that comes with such foods.

"We'll have to meet for lunch one day," she said. "I'm with a law firm in One Shell Square."

42

The pleasure I took in her foodstuffs lasted just a little less time than the pleasure I found in her humility of not announcing that she was an attorney until the last moment. But of course she was not an attorney at all, not a person who, at least by social judgments, was allowed to hold forth on any subject just because she had three years of complicated schooling above the bachelor's degree. Caroline was a legal secretary, as I found out when she scheduled lunch around her allotted one hour at noon. But then she had never actually said she was a lawyer.

"The red beans and hot sausage on Mondays is perfect here," she said, then closed the menu. I thought she expected me to close mine, but I continued to read.

"You saw the morning paper," she said, and I looked up. "I am so sick with it."

I looked at her with confusion. There was a lot in the morning paper, most not worth reading unless a person had a need for the absurd. The headlines never made sense; the stories were always distorted. Whatever was actually happening in the world was never reported, squeezed out by accounts of malfeasance at every level of public officialdom. Our governor was under indictment for racketeering; half of our police force, at any given time, seemed to be teetering between charges of manslaughter and first degree murder for taking their job perks, the sheer free pleasure of brutalizing hopped up, angry, cop-baiting black boys.

"They tore up the cemetery," she said.

"Our cemetery?" I thought I would have known.

"Our cemetery?" she said. "Oh, you mean *your* cemetery, the one by your house."

"Well, your dog craps all over it," I said. I thought Caroline was the type to hate such language, but she smiled.

"Where my father's buried, Lafayette Number One." Where my dog had run off to, probably peeing on tombs, evening the score.

"I'm sorry," I told her. I pictured spray paint, TROY40ANGELA, broken copping. I pictured angry boys, walking through the cream of the Garden District, on their way to the shack rows near the river, giving the ultimate insult. Mess the graveyard; even the dead in New Orleans are not democratic.

"A bunch of rich kids, thought they were so precious. Just foolish desecration, digging up dry bones, playing nasty little rituals out in front of one another. You know, candles dripping and calla lilies and black robes and whatever we all thought was so clever at that age. But they went too far. Though I guess their parents will buy them out of trouble, as long as they didn't drip candle wax all over their own great-grandfathers' skulls."

I started to laugh, but Caroline didn't even crack the smallest smile. The waiter came, and she ordered us both the red beans and rice with sausage. I found myself choking through the rest of the hour, waiting to see whether she would offer to pay for my food. I would have chosen something less opaque to eat.

"Rolla's adopting Liana week after next," she said. "Her father took off when she was a baby; just couldn't take it."

Just couldn't take you, I wanted to say. I said nothing. I was too curious, in spite of myself.

"I know what I've done," she said. "You have your first child when you're almost forty, you know what might happen. Everything I've done with Liana, it's in case I'm not there one day."

I looked at her queerly. That's an issue of having babies, of not outliving them. I couldn't imagine thinking about it for more than the time it takes for the notion to come and go. "Liana can go anywhere with anyone. She knows what to say in any situation."

"How dreadful," I said.

"Why?" If I'd thought Caroline would find my remark funny, I probably wouldn't have made it.

"I just prefer a little ambiguity in my life. You should be able to tell that," I said, and she smiled.

Caroline paid the check after all, and I was ready to go at her again for more. It was the tiniest of concessions at the end of each meeting that brought me back into seeing her each time. Leave them sated or laughing.

It didn't take Caroline long to die, now that I look back at it. Seven months is very little time, unless of course it is woven in and out of phases of promise. Caroline's self-aware-

45

ness was as keen as a CAT scan, better even, as it turned out. I never touched the nodal parts of my own body, never saw the sclera and melanin in enough light to be frightened, but Caroline knew it all. She found the metastasis, three grand schoolboy marbles in her neck, just a week after Andy Shaskan's medical school drinking buddies in nuclear medicine had given Caroline a clean bill of health. They saw no need to look up that high. It was probably Andy's fault, but I guess when he was only a few weeks off Caroline could not have sued him.

Caroline worked at her own salvation with the ignorant arrogance that had always made her feel so excellent. She took Vitamin E and started a macrobiotic diet just three weeks after she had slogged herself full of red beans and sausage. And she alternated between saving herself and preparing a world for Liana without her.

"I read that aluminum may play a role in Alzheimer's," she said. "I've quit using deodorant." She smelled only of the onions that she ate, never of uncleanliness after that. When it moved into her brain, she went first to her dentist for the headaches. "He wants to recap all my teeth," she said. "Can you imagine? He said to come back in six months. Six months!"

And she began to buy me. At Christmas, Sarie received slips and earrings and tiny fine pencils from Liana. I would not have gone shopping on a death sentence.

"Liana will need mothering," she said at other times, in an abstracted way, so that I could not absolutely point at her and say that she was getting me ready for a new responsibility.

She never told Liana, not until the week before she died. Liana became mopey and queer, always off in a corner, reading a book, never turning a page. We had her for days when Caroline was in the hospital, and Liana never thought to say that she was frightened. She went to her violin lessons as if it were never a possibility to fight a glut of culture her mother wanted to last past a lifetime. Tending Liana took more running time than tending a regular child. When there was free time, she went off to the sidelines, and she did a lot of watching, I thought.

Rolla began slipping into motherhood. The weekend before Caroline died, he took the girls to see *The Wizard of Oz*. It was playing in a nine o'clock slot, and no one else was in the theater.

"Mr. Conn sang 'Ding dong the witch is dead' like Donald Duck," Sarie said, doubling over with breathless fits. He let them run up and down the aisles and fed them six kinds of candy and took them out for pizza afterwards, and I thought of how long he was going to pay for violin lessons.

Rolla rang our bell during supper Monday night. "She's gone," he said. I asked him to come in. "I haven't told the kid yet," he said.

47

At the church Liana floated with a certain lovely pleasure. She wore white eyelet lace, pressed fresh, white tights, brand-new black patent leather shoes. She had fixed her own hair in two quite fine pigtails. And while Rolla stood at the door of the church gauging the mood, murmuring sadnesses to some and telling the joke about the Sewerage and Water Board to others, Liana worked the crowd, too. "She looks yellow and not real," she warned us when we arrived. "My dad told me I wouldn't think it was her." She walked us up to the front as if showing off her prize sculpture at the school art show. Then she drifted off, the consummate hostess, bringing the next visitor up to see her mother, rattling off the same spiel.

I saw Andy Shaskan come in and edged toward the back of the church, perhaps hoping that I would work up the nerve to say something. Andy looked ten years older than I thought he should. He was almost completely bald; like many doctors his only sensuality probably now lay behind the closed examining room door. I watched Rolla greet him as I approached. There was just the smallest bit of contrition in Andy's expression.

"Better luck next time," Rolla said in his Donald Duck voice. I turned to go sit down, afraid I would begin laughing so hard that I would not be able to stop.

I was not the only one who watched Liana, I'm sure. It's probably a natural and morbid thing to do, a learning experience. But Liana was quite boring at the church, acquiescing to Rolla's sob-racked hug as they reached the

48

pew, well-rehearsed, indifferent. She was quite boring during the service, just sitting distractedly as if it were a regular Sunday morning. I could picture her reaching for a book, pulling back with disdain from the rituals that were for everyone else.

She and Rolla rode in the limousine to the cemetery, even though the Lafayette Number One Cemetery was only four blocks from the church on the avenue. Everyone else walked. It was a warm March afternoon, four o'clock so that all Liana's school friends could be there. Caroline's idea.

Someone had given Liana sunglasses. She looked very beautiful in them, a striking woman's face with those pigtails and that ballet-class body. I looked around for the desecration, discreetly. Probably everyone else was looking, too, even though all signs should have been gone by then, if anyone had thought about it. The burial was in her father's tomb; Caroline's mother was living, and Caroline had no dead husbands yet. It was crowded, the way it usually is in those stone villages that pass for graveyards in places where the dead have to be buried above ground because of the rising water table. Alfred said that you can bury a person in a raised family plot once every six years; that's how long it takes for the predecessor to sink down toward the center of the earth. He knows a lot, such as what rots first.

The minister rolled up and down his own intonations, and I looked at Liana. She was standing by herself in front of the group of adults positioned opposite me. Rolla was at the graveside. And Liana just stood there, the huge sunglasses at a jaunty, sensual angle on her nose. She was smiling. Not show-off smiling, not sun-avoiding. Just smiling.

Previously published in *Above Ground* and *Something in the Water*, and used with permission.

PASSING AT LE HAVRE

I should have suspected something when my father reduced the Holocaust to a simple, Hardyesque little romance. "Your mother and I, we probably saw each other. Just brushed past, you know." That was about all he told of those years, and I imagined that scene until it crammed enough into itself to make sense. He was sharp and trim, a superlative sort who was getting out when maybe others didn't quite merit it as much; why else? I saw him in my mind's eye with a small valise that carried a silver esrog box, two gold coins, and a change of underwear. The box and the coins were all he had from the time before he came over. I put the evidence together.

51

With my mother, Letty, it was much easier. There are many photographs of her from that time. Black-and-white photographs, but I can imagine Letty in color. Her Persian lamb coat, her reddish-gold curls, unkempt, a puff of a rich girl, just wafting behind her own mother, with absolutely no sense of history. I picture my grandmother with a cigarette dangling from her mouth. For no particular reason, except it seemed like a damned cavalier thing to do, and I know my grandmother smoked from the time she was fifteen.

When my grandmother — I called her Marmee — took me to Europe in 1961, I didn't see Le Havre, probably for a reason no one ever thought of hard enough to bring to the surface. The *Liberte* dropped Marmee and me off at Southampton. It didn't dock, just deposited us on a smaller boat that ferried us in. We made it across Europe by other means, a plane to Amsterdam, a train to Paris, a car with a driver to take us into the Swiss Alps. So the one time I went to Europe I never saw Le Havre. But I saw pieces of Marmee's 1939 trip with Letty. Like the opera house in Paris. Rich with history, the opera house was full of Marmee's own story, too. She took me to a spot under the grand staircase.

"Here's where I read Letty the cable from your grandfather," she said. "'Get out of Europe immediately,' it said. She and I just laughed. They were doing *Faust* that night, too."

For years after that I wondered how, in 1939, or in any

other year for that matter, they managed to get a telegram delivered to my grandmother at the opera. Finally, I asked Letty. "Oh, it came to the hotel. She just chucked it into her purse and waited until intermission to open it." They didn't take it very seriously, Letty agreed; they had to see the rest of the opera, of course, and they still had a lot of shopping to do.

Marmee probably got a number of bargains those last few days in Europe, as the center was about to fail to hold. She was still a terrific shopper in 1961, when she took me. A platinum watch, as thin as an eggshell for my grandfather; fine linen suits, covered in embroidery, for me, suits that made me look like an unrefrigerated prune after a few hours of squirming around in some vehicle, looking out of the window to get Marmee's money's worth; queer copper luster pieces and a real Rouault for herself.

I kept waiting for a global drama to unfold, something that would take me back home and away from the civilizing influences of my grandmother. She watched my food, she had my hair and nails trimmed in every capital, she made me read the guides and pamphlets until all the fresh excitement was wrung out of a place before I got there. But nothing happened in the world to take me back; Hemingway committed suicide when we were in Montreux, but I could see that that struck no particular fear in Marmee. She just kept shopping and touring, and we took a plane back to the States from Athens. We never made it back full circle to the European ports of entry along the Atlantic.

After a month home the polish had worn off of me. The linen suits were all on hangers, yes, but at the back of my closet, never cleaned or ironed. The ends of my hair were uneven, and my fingernails were grown out shapeless. What happened to the girl who came off the plane? my father asked. I couldn't read his tone, I couldn't tell at all if he was mocking what I now saw as pretension, or if he was just a little sorry, having had illusions all along that I was going to be a rich puff of a girl, as Letty had been, trailing along the quais, maybe fanning away some of the cigarette smoke drifting behind her mother. She was sixteen, and he liked to believe he had seen her.

No, it all wore off, even the learning. After a while I no longer knew in what century Louis XIV lived, what decade *Faust* was written in, what year the Archduke Ferdinand was shot in. But I did know the day my mother and my father were at the docks in Le Havre, each waiting to take one of the two remaining ships out of Europe. I knew the date before I got on the boat with Marmee, and I came back knowing the date.

I hated it, I told Letty. I'm just not the sort she wants me to be. I want to be simple, not to broadcast anything when I'm out. She didn't do anything permanent to you, for God's sake, Letty said. And then she laughed. A private joke with herself. What's so funny? I asked her.

"When my grandmother tried *her* style of culture on me," she said, "she left long-term effects." I looked at her quizzically. That would have been my great-grandmother,

54

who died when I was four. I remembered her, I thought, though she came up often enough in conversations and photographs that maybe she was just another of my fantasy constructions. She wore deep purple all the time, incipient schizophrenia, a sure sign, was the way Letty interpreted it for as long as the subject came up. And it still comes up, every time deep purple is in fashion. Though probably it wasn't when my great-grandmother wore it. A rich lady, no doubt, because Marmee lived well on inherited money; my great-grandmother was not too aware of her wealth.

"She took me to the stockyards when I visited her in Chicago," Letty said. "And she bought me chocolate candy after the tour. Right at the stockyards she bought it. I swear it tasted like the stench of the place, and I couldn't eat chocolate for years after that."

Marmee and I bought a lot of chocolate in Europe. In Scheveningen I got hot chocolate every morning with my breakfast. Creamy and sweet. And cheeses and thin, pale ham, dry toast triangles and real butter. After a while I got used to the richness of the food. I even expected it. But the trip wasn't long enough for me to get arrogant, to go on expecting exquisite treatment because we had a lot of money to spend. Marmee barked at the serving people, the waiters, the hotel clerks, the drivers. Her time was very valuable, and they simply were not supposed to waste it.

It was still very hot most of the time that September when I was eleven. I had gotten to the point where my trip with

Marmee two months before was a lavish bad dream. She was back to being my grandmother in familiar contexts, abusing only those people whose names I knew, Letty, her city housekeeper Murray, my grandfather. They all loved her, of course, and I imagined I would develop adult mechanisms to be insensitive to that kind of self-centeredness — one day. So I didn't mind the notion of being with her, without the buffer of my parents, and I was fairly pleased when, just after school had started, she offered to take me along on one of their weekends at Pass Christian.

You have to ask your father, Letty said when I told her of the call from Marmee. It was a funny kind of permission to have to ask for; I really didn't understand it. I could see the value of mulling over whether I could sleep over at a friend's house when the friend had a mother newly divorced and a little wacky with it. I could understand needing permission to bicycle to the pharmacy: I had to cross two fast lanes right past a river-following curve in the avenue. Grandparents didn't seem to represent hazards. They had raised Letty to responsibility, intact.

I let her ask my father. That was her request: I'll talk it over with him after he's had dinner and a chance to relax a little. That would make it after ten, after I was asleep. He was a manager at Marino's supermarket. We live on your grandmother's money, Letty made sure to tell me whenever an expenditure seemed to exceed what was reasonable to expect from a family headed by the manager of a supermarket. My father always worked until eight on weeknights, though in those days the store closed at six-thirty.

For a while I believed he had been saved that day in Le Havre. It was a perfect little tale, the way he told it; it never took him more than ten minutes to run through it all.

"Nobody believed anything could go so wrong, you know. My mother was a superstitious old Jewess, that type. Maybe she would have been smart if she had been born now, but then she was just flighty and foolish. That was the word in the street. No one believed what was happening. But I was working for the American government there. They were actually succeeding in getting Jews out of the camps, and they could use me. Use me well. I was twenty-three, a bit of a bohemian, wild enough to take those sorts of risks. They said get out. I took my mother's word for days, but they got more and more emphatic, and one day I believed them. My mother wouldn't come. So I had to tell her goodbye."

At that point I always began to cry. Matter-of-fact, he just said it matter-of-fact, but it was like any familiar story when you know the ending. "I got the last train to the border. The SS came on board, and you know, for some reason I had had the good sense to bury those gold coins in a bar of soap. A bar of soap! They would have killed me for less. But I got out, the last train to Paris. The last of two ships left at Le Havre. Your mother and I, we probably bumped into each other. Just brushed past."

But he really wasn't saved, not when all it came to was keeping the shelves stocked for the rich ladies of uptown, and keeping the poor cashiers, who often lived right around the corner from the rich ladies, content and pleased enough with his democratic ways not to quit.

"They're trying to turn my daughter into someone I don't like."

I could hear him through the wall. Usually I was asleep by ten, but I'd been straining to stay awake to know his decision. I could leave school at noon on Friday for such an excursion; I'd been allowed to do it once before. I didn't want to wait until morning, having to creep into the kitchen and try to read Letty's expression before finding out.

"Darby foils them," Letty said with a tinkly, conspiratorial sort of laugh.

"You don't know how she'll turn out. Darby could go either way. I don't like these dizzy, spoiled women here."

"My mother's oppressive. Anyone with any sense rebels. I did. You've managed to live with me." There was almost a seductive tone in her voice, though then seduction to me had nothing to do with anything but getting one's own way.

"Well, I'm certainly not going to forbid her to go. I let her go to Europe, I'll let her go across the lake. Making it off-limits would only make it appealing. I know better."

It got quiet, and though I thought I would sleep well, I seemed just to coast on the cusp of sleep the rest of the night. It occurred to me that maybe I wanted to make a decision

58

about going with my grandparents, but I couldn't quite weigh the good against the bad. The good was the last sun of the summer; even if there was no one else on the beach, I could run at the waves. There were smells on the beach that I remembered from when I was too small to walk, and those smells gave me a most terrific sense of well-being. And staying at a place housing my grandmother was totally indulgent.

She had an old Cajun woman who lived in the house to tend it during weekdays, when Marmee was back in the city harassing Murray, and on weekends the woman cooked and cleaned and even made the beds. I just couldn't figure out the bad parts, the abstractions that might not even amount to anything. I finally fell asleep when I knew that letting my father decide was the wisest course.

My grandfather had a white Lincoln, a sleek car with sharp, angular tail fins. I thought it was the most elegant car on the road that year. But even at eleven I knew that the way he drove was sometimes not quite right. I didn't put it together until years afterwards that his drinking was connected with it. When we drove across the lake he maneuvered adequately. It was the middle of the day. He had put in four good hours at his law office; my grandfather was a lazy sort of maritime attorney who whiled away his days when he felt like it, sure in the knowledge that he did not need to work, much less succeed. But on Sunday evening, when we came back, he was wobbly at the wheel, yet strikingly self-assured. Marmee seemed not to notice. She just stewed over last week's *New York Times* crossword, watching the roadway only occasionally, when carsick from the concentration, needing to get grounded back in space. The car was full of smoke from her cigarettes.

I was riding in the backseat. For me that was unusual, because up until the time we went to Europe, I always had ridden stretched across the rear-window shelf. Before I turned eleven and became a world traveler, I never stopped much to think that I was quite a visible spectacle, scrunched up there in plain sight of any cars following us. I just enjoyed doing what I knew was a bad thing, something my father never let me do. I always had managed to slink down from out of there when we approached our house. Even when I was very small and didn't know streets. But now I was just urbane as hell, arrogant in my own way, and full of those first rushes of self-consciousness that come as a girl's body starts to change.

So I was riding on the backseat, more comfortable than I'd ever been in one of their cars, to tell the truth. The sun began to set, and I was full of rich food and puffed with Gulf-water salt and burned from hot sun on overcast days. I fell asleep, and as the car danced down the highway I worked my way around in my sleep until I was stretched happily across the seat, my head bumping up against my small overnight case, every muscle loose and trusting.

Something happened to jolt me out of sleep, and by the time I was clear enough to sit up and open my eyes, we were parked alongside the highway. It was dark out, and the cars kept zipping by us. Traffic was heavy heading in our direction, though few cars were going the opposite way, from the city to the beach. There was a small filling station maybe a hundred yards ahead of us, and there were two rusty advertisements planted just past the car.

My grandfather was at the wheel, but Marmee had gotten out. I lay back down, to see what would happen, and I saw her come back and tell him to get out. I waited for what seemed like hours, not feeling abandoned because there seemed to be a lot of activity around the car. When I saw a flashing red light, I peered over and saw a police car. Frightened, I lay back down again. Then I heard a siren, but I didn't get up. It came toward us, it stopped, time passed, and it started up again, tearing away from us.

Whatever happened, we certainly weren't detained long. I stayed supine on the backseat, not letting on that I had been awake for anything. For quite a while, they said nothing to each other, each just looking straight forward. It was nighttime now, and Marmee had nothing to amuse herself, but still she didn't talk to my grandfather.

"He's going to live, for Chrissake," my grandfather finally said. "They told you he's going to be all right."

"I just feel funny, that's all," Marmee said.

"It was his goddamn fault. Even the police told you he was drunk. Just walking along, as drunk as he could be. It was his fault."

"You think we should have done something?"

"Like what?"

"Well, he wasn't exactly a half-dead dog on the side of the road."

"Naw, he was a drunk, half-dead dog on the side of the road," my grandfather said, and they both laughed.

Of course, these were the only grandparents I ever knew, and maybe they weren't half-bad, but I had little point of real comparison.

"I'm a lucky woman, I've never had to contend with in-law troubles," Letty used to say, and when she said it in front of my father he always looked at her queerly. But his look didn't deter her from coming out with it again. All I knew of my other grandparents was a single black-and-white photograph my father kept in that silver esrog box, right on top of the English drop-leaf desk, seventeenth century, in the living room. I had heard Marmee say it was tacky, inappropriate there.

"For a Jewish woman, you sure are anti-Semitic," Letty had said back.

Fiddling around the desk, I found the photograph when I was very small, though I was almost grown before I knew what it actually meant. It was a double grave, two stones. And on the one with my grandmother's name it said, at the bottom 16-3-1943 NACH THERESIENSTADT. My parents were married in the summer of 1941, and once I called Letty on that fact. You had a mother-in-law for almost two years, I told her. Well, hardly, she said, the poor woman was trapped over there. She showed me a bundle of letters, all in German, and all I could interpret was the postmarks. They started in January of 1940, and they stopped in August of 1942. Letty didn't know a word of German, but I guessed she remembered the letters coming; some of the later ones had a New Orleans address. "Trapped," she said, brandishing the bundle at me, then shrugging a little sadly and shoving them into a desk drawer. It was the drawer next to the one they kept their tax papers in, and it was otherwise empty.

"What the hell happened to you?" my father said as I walked up the front path. My grandparents were in the car in the driveway, the motor idling, knowing better than to get out. But my father was deliberately loud, his accent thick and funny with the idiom of twenty years' accumulation not quite rolling off his tongue. He signaled to my grandfather to come in, and my grandfather stepped out of the car with that sort of swagger a man has when he's just bought off a policeman or two. That wasn't enough. He signaled again, and I could see the fretful annoyance in her movements as Marmee reached over and cut off the lights and the ignition.

"It was a bad accident, but we're all right," my grandfather said before my father could say another word, before Marmee could even get halfway up the walk.

"A man, badly injured." Marmee was dramatic, breathless.

"So why didn't you call? We were worried sick." So many Ws in his sentence. My poor father.

"From the side of the goddamn highway?"

"You didn't go to a hospital, a police station, something?"

"You know how these things go," my grandfather said, remembering to be pleased with himself and forgetting to be circumspect with everyone else.

"You paid your way out, you bastard," my father screamed. We were still not in the house. I was still not shooed away.

"It can be done," Marmee said sweetly.

"And twenty years ago? Where was all the money then? When I needed you? It could have been done. I saw the American government setting it up in Stuttgart every goddamn day. You could have gotten my mother out!" I recoiled: the Holocaust had been nothing more than a romantic passing at Le Havre, and quietly told tales of saying good-bye to the grandmother I'd never met. My father had kept his past awfully well concealed, at least to an eleven-year-old.

He was frantic, and I could see the vein at his temple swelled to the point of bursting. "You could have done it," he said softly.

I went up to my room. Marmee had made me promise at the beach that I would shampoo my hair and shape my nails when I got home. I had salt in my hair, my clothes were acrid with sweat and Gulf water. I didn't undress, I just fell into bed as plain as I could be, and when the porch light went out I fell asleep.

Reprinted from *The Xavier Review* (later a chapter in *The Exact Image of Mother*)

TWO-STORY BRICK HOUSES

You only need two things to feel good at Newman School, Pappagallos that show your toe crack and a two-story brick house. Well, three things if you're Jewish. If you're Jewish you have to go to Sunday school. I don't have any of those things, but I can fake the third one. Thirty-seven out of sixty-two kids in my class at Newman are Jewish if you count Carolyn and Shira, and strangely enough, you don't think about them as being Jewish *because* they had bas mitzvahs. They also came from public school in seventh grade and are fat and don't care. It was Carolyn, who goes to a synagogue I've never heard of, who told me just to say that I go to Gates of Prayer. It's reform, but nobody's ever heard of it.

I keep working on my mother to buy me Pappagallos, but she

says I get my shoes free and I should brag about it instead of mope. My great-grandfather owned the Imperial Shoe Store which is on the corner of Bourbon and Canal Streets, and my grandfather gets such a deep discount that he buys all my shoes. Imperial is one of those stores that sells sturdy shoes like Stride-Rite. Okay, but I don't understand why they waited until Capezios went out of style to get them in. I can have all the Capezios I want, now that I don't want them.

I don't think we're poor, but I can't really tell. We live in a house that's actually old and pretty, but it's wood and one-story so it doesn't even matter that my grandmother pays for us to have a maid. Well, she pays twenty-five dollars a week, but after a while Rena wanted a raise, and my grandmother said no, so my father pays her extra every week, taking it out of what he would spend on dry cleaning his suit. That's the way it is with my grandparents.

My grandmother paid my tuition to Newman for kindergarten, and then she said she didn't feel like it anymore, so I've been on scholarship ever since. Which means my daddy has to reveal his income every year. Newman is very low-key about it, but my mother's not. I have to have very good grades. Which is pretty easy because this is more a school for rich kids than for smart kids in spite of what the whole city thinks. I know for a fact that if your parents knew the admissions director when you were coming into kindergarten, she asked you which train was red, and which one was black, and if you got it right, you were in. She came from a very old Jewish family and had nothing better to do than give admissions tests for Newman. She still does it.

There's a slumber party at Louise Silverman's house tonight,

67

and I'm invited. I have been at this school for over ten years, and this is the first time I'm friends with all the snobbish girls. My mother is thrilled, and I am disgusted, but I'm also thrilled, to tell the truth. Louise lives on Octavia Street, and two of the other girls actually can walk to her house. Their houses look almost the same, and I think that's a message to me that if you want to be the right kind of person, then you should have that kind of house. Brick two-story. A plain rectangle. My mother probably thinks so, too, but my father is the manager of a supermarket, and she knows crummy shoes and Rena's twenty-five dollars a week is probably her limit with her parents.

Louise and Meryl and both of the Lindas are failing Geometry. For a while they took turns calling me up for homework help, then I started going over to their houses after school, and finally they quit pretending they could do anything without me. This is how I know people at Newman aren't smart. For homework for Monday we have to prove the congruence of the two triangles in a parallelogram. I'm going over to Louise's early, and we're going to work on it. She'll just hand it over to the other three. They won't be able to do it in Mrs. Walter's class when she comes at them, and they won't be able to do it on tests, and from what I've heard Mrs. Prescott will threaten them with public school, but at homework time they will think I'm giving them hope.

My mother has packed me my gold silk pajamas that my grandmother bought me on her last trip to Japan. "Those girls are going to be so jealous," she says. I think there's a chance she might be right, though I also think that gold silk shoes from Japan would not hold up next to nice baby-blue leather Pappagallos. I ask her to drop me off and not wait until someone opens the door. We have a

1956 Ford Fairlane sedan. I figure that if no one opens the door I can go ring another girl's bell. It is better than being seen in a 1956 Ford Fairlane sedan.

Louise grabs my arm at the door and pulls me in, which is as close as she comes to affection. "We'll do math right now," she says, and I think she must know that I'm excited, too, by an idea I've come up with on the way over. If Mrs. Silverman sees this little lesson I've made up for Louise, she will decide I am the best girl in all of Newman School and should be the only one Louise should be friends with. She might tell all the other mothers, and then I'll be popular. These girls aren't like me. They definitely plan to grow up to be just like their mothers.

While I pull my math book out of my overnight bag, I ask Louise to get me a couple of envelopes, please. She looks at me like I've asked her to get me cleaning supplies. This is not something she's ever found necessary. "Mama!" she hollers, and goes running upstairs. Her mother comes down to the kitchen and rummages in a drawer in the butler's pantry. These two-story brick houses fascinate me. They have rooms that make sense only for rich people who lived a hundred years ago, but they were built ten years ago. I ask for scissors, too. Louise's maid stands at the sink watching us with her arms folded. She's not doing anything but watching us. Her expression says she could do this geometry if someone asked her.

My wish comes true: Mrs. Silverman watches as I cut and fold and draw straight lines and prove beyond doubt the congruence of the triangles in a parallelogram. I even cut the envelope into the shape of a parallelogram despite the fact that a rectangle is a sort of parallelogram, because I figure Louise and her mother aren't going to follow that extra piece of information. They are as delighted as if I've just guessed which card they've pulled from a deck. Mrs. Silverman kisses my cheek with red lips, and I leave the mark because no other girl is going to have a print to match Mrs. Silverman tonight.

***

The maid is still standing at the sink around midnight when I pad into the kitchen to find a way not to cry. We are in our nightclothes, and everyone in her pink shortie pajamas has said how pretty my pajamas are and has examined the little frog buttons closely so she can comment when I leave the room. Silk is so hot, and I don't want to have perspiration stains under my arms. They will show so easily. I don't feel sorry for myself. I really don't. I feel sorry for Carolyn, who of course is not here. I feel sorry for the maid. I feel sorry for everybody. I must look pitiful.

"What a big old girl like you doing in baby nightclothes?" the maid says.

"They're from *Japan*," I say like a white person, and I suddenly don't feel so bad.

Louise is the one making the calls. They are calling Negro cab companies and sending taxis to Carolyn's house. "How you doin'?" she says, trying to sound colored. I think she sounds fifteen and stupid, but everyone else thinks it's hysterical and is laughing into a pillow. "Yeah, I just got off work, you could pick me up?" She rifles through the school directory. This is why she's flunking math. She can't even

70

hold Carolyn's address in her head for two minutes. When she hangs up, they all start screeching with laughter.

"I thought you liked Negroes," I whisper. Though right now I hate her maid.

Louise looks around to see whether she does or not. She draws blank stares. We all took Civics last year and Mr. Ralph taught us to love President Kennedy, and now all the girls except me have giant hair rollers on their heads so they can look like Mrs. Kennedy in the morning. That is supposed to mean we like Negroes. I explain that to Louise, and she agrees. She has a picture of him in her room. Rena has one in her kitchen, but I've never told Louise that. President Kennedy is very good-looking, she says, but why am I asking about Negroes?

Because it's their cabs.

Oh, says Linda B., they're out anyway. We'll make Carolyn crazy. Remember Teal? I remember Teal. They called her all night every night until she was driven to public school in sixth grade.

And I think, I have a feeling *you* are going to be sitting in public school when Carolyn is up there in Trigonometry at Newman. I'm having a good time. I'm inside my own head, but I like being in their company.

Linda B. is the one who makes the calls to Carolyn's house. She thinks she can do a voice deep enough to be a boy our age, and she asks for Carolyn. "Oh, God, she used the F word and all kinds of Jewish words," Linda says, covering the receiver. "What's a shwotzer?"

"It's *schwartzer*," I say, "and it's a derogatory word for Negroes."

Then I realize they are going to think I'm Jewish the way Carolyn and Shira are, so I have to explain really fast that if they paid attention to the way words are derived they'd notice that there are people at school named Schwartz, and that means "black," so it's just a form of a German word. I don't mention that my father is from Germany, and that he's been secretly teaching me German since I was three years old. Well, talking to me in German. You don't *teach* a child. My mother doesn't know.

All the girls trip all over themselves telling me how smart I am. I think this is different from my pajamas. This is not something they are going to talk about differently when I leave the room. I am smart, and that fact is unassailably good, and in their presence I am better than they are no matter what subject comes up, as long as it isn't fashion.

When it seems that Carolyn has been tormented as close to going back to public school as is possible for one night, Linda R. says we need to play Secrets. Louise dims the lights, and we sit in a circle, and we drink Coke. There are eight of us, and we're going clockwise, and since we started with Meryl, I have three people ahead of me before I have to think up something to tell. I figure I'll decide on the basis of what they tell. My father likes to have what he calls private jokes with himself. I want to think up a private joke with myself. If I can think of a secret that they think is something they can hold against me, but really is something I can use against them, it'll be a lot of fun.

Of course Meryl has a crush on our English teacher and she had a dream last week that she went down to his French Quarter apartment and had sex with him. This is a complete lie. People don't have night dreams that everyone in the room has daydreams about, especially when nobody really wants to do anything more with that man than kiss him. I pick this apart in my head. It's a secret about *her*, and it's one people can use in the halls. Louise tells that Becca in her fourth period French class came right out in the girls' bathroom and said that her parents got a divorce because her mother was having an affair, not her father, even though it's always the father who fucks around.

Becca is an atheist, and Becca doesn't care if she has any friends, but boys call her up anyway because she has huge breasts. She tells them no and goes out with Tulane boys. I'm not sure what to do with this for the purposes of tonight, but I am sure what to do with it for life in general.

I'm going to quit pretending I'm anything but an atheist. My father hasn't said so, but I know he's one. He won't affiliate with a synagogue because he says synagogues in New Orleans are really just churches without crucifixes. I think he's just figured out that this God thing makes no sense. I know I have.

When it's my turn, something makes me tell that I speak German. It will be a private joke with myself. Linda B. says I have to say something, and I say, *"Du bist boese and haesslich,"* which means *You are mean and ugly*, but I tell them it means, *You are smart and beautiful*. Linda says it sounds like the way Carolyn's mother talks, and everyone else chimes in, agreeing. Carolyn's mother throws in maybe one word that sounds sort of German, I tell them, and they mull that over for a while, ask me to say something else.

I take it on as a parlor trick: they ask for *Boys think I'm sexy,* and I give them back, *"Maenner denken I rieche wie Pferdescheisse,"* which means, *Boys think I smell like horse shit.* Linda wants to know how I know how to speak German when I've been sitting in Newman all these years with all of them, and Newman hasn't taught it to me. My father's from Germany, I tell them. No, he's not, they say. Nazis are from Germany. They start looking at me hard. My last name is Cooper. That's not a Jewish name. It's not a German name. It was Kuper until my father got to Ellis Island. I shouldn't have to explain this. "I'm Jewish, for Chrissakes," I say, which I think is a pretty good joke, but they don't get it. "How do we know you're not a Nazi?" Linda says.

"Because my grandmother was killed by the Nazis," I say. I want to go home.

They all get quiet for a moment. They all have grandmothers who are just like their mothers.

Finally Louise, who is in my European History class and getting a B without cheating, says, "If the Nazis killed her, how can she be your grandmother when she was dead before you were born? I mean, the war ended in, what, 1945?"

"Because my father had a mother, and that's how you have a grandmother, no matter what," I say. I'm feeling better. Newman is a remarkable school. All of these girls will go on to college. Though some are going to take a detour through public school.

"Prove it," Louise says.

And I tell them, "There's a bundle of letters in my parents' bottom desk drawer." I can read every one. In German. Right up to the very end. When she was taken to the camps.

***

Mrs. Prescott has done the math for the mothers, and this six weeks is going to require As from all four of those girls just to get Ds. At that Mrs. Prescott has said she's not sure any of them is what she calls Newman material. Meryl says that Newman material also has a lot to do with donations to the school, and her father is going to give five thousand dollars, and there's probably a secret formula that mixes grades with parents' contributions, so she's not worried. But she must have some kind of dignity problem, because she's not willing to come out of tenth grade with an F in Geometry, and that means I'm still going to have four friends at least until June. Meryl says we should have a slumber party at my house.

If people are going to come to my party, I want to have it, and I want to have it just the way they would. My mother won't have Rena spend the night, and when I think about it, I'm relieved but angry anyway. She also won't buy me shortie pajamas. So I cut the legs and sleeves off my silk pajamas and make very good hems in them, and there's not a thing my mother can do. There's also not a thing the other girls can say because the truth is that my pajamas are really better than theirs. At least I hope they are. My mother lets me have Coke. She doesn't know that Coke and Oreos are right while Pepsi and Hydrox are wrong. Daddy knows, and he's not telling. He doesn't think I should have to squirm through life. But there's no way to tell that to my mother because she likes to see me squirm. At least that's the way it looks to me.

When my very cute house is quiet, and we're all sitting around in my very cute living room, Linda R. looks at my parents' desk and says, "So, is that their desk?" As if it is a peculiar kind of furniture found only in some obscure foreign country. Which to most of them it might be. I haven't seen desks in most of their houses. Or bookshelves. I tell her yes. "So is that where you found the letters from the lady that got killed by the Nazis?"

I tell her yes.

Linda R. crawls right over to the desk and opens the bottom drawer. It's the drawer where we keep all our memorabilia. Very neatly. My baby book, my mother's baby book. A scrapbook of photos and an envelope of more photos. My mother's diploma and my father's honorable discharge from the U.S. Army, which he got four years and two months after he left Germany. And the packet of letters, which always lies nestled in the lower right-hand corner at the front. It's impossible to miss, and Linda doesn't miss it. She plucks it out without the tenderness a person should afford these pages and pages of aerogramme paper, thin as onionskin.

"Be careful with that," is all I can think to say. She undoes the ribbon, and they cascade to the floor. I leap to take them before they can fall out of order. I have read them, but I've read them like a detective who doesn't want even fingerprints left behind. Linda pulls back, offended, as if I've called her a slob.

"Hey, I just want you to read us one. Read it in *German*."

Of course the one on the top of the stack is the last one, the most frantic one. My grandmother has seen the light now that it is too late. She is writing to my father in New York, sorry she didn't listen to him when he said they had to leave. My father has enlisted in the military to survive.

"I think you know people on Park Avenue," she says. "People on Park Avenue have money. I understand you can still buy a way to America. Please ask your friends for help. I don't know why I don't hear from you."

I read it in German. I translate without playing around.

77

"God, she didn't get it, did she," Meryl says.

"Did your dad really know a lot of rich people?" Louise says.

I don't say anything.

"Well, how come your father didn't just go over and *get* her?" Louise says. "I mean, just get on a plane or something? That's what I'd've done."

I tell her it was 1943. That ought to connote more than the fact that commercial air travel didn't exist, but it probably doesn't.

Louise says, "So what happened next?" She is far too excited. "She fucking died in a concentration camp," I say. I fold the letter back and put it in its envelope and reassemble the packet of letters so it's impossible to tell they've been touched. I put them back in the drawer. I go to sleep hours before they have their fill of Coke and meanness.

***

Mrs. Prescott comes to take me out of Geometry class, and Mrs. Walter makes her wait until the end of the period; such is her power. I'm not bothered until she tells me she's taking me home. This is not something Mrs. Prescott would do; it's too generous. People who work at Newman are not generous because they would be destroyed by the children. She protects herself, saying nothing in the car, and when we approach my house and I see my grandparents' car and a police car, she doesn't do anything except say that someone will get me my homework. I have to walk in alone.

This morning, an hour before Geometry class, my father killed himself in his office.

He found a bag made of plastic in the store, put it tight over his head, and waited to die. The policeman has a manila envelope with some evidence in it that he wants me to look at. Everyone in the room is wide-eyed and dry-eyed, and I'm supposed to be that way, too, but I bawl like a baby, and I can't look at stupid evidence, and I don't know who they think I am. I see Rena standing by the wall, and her eyes are wet and red. She loves my father. He always jokes with her, tries to use a southern accent and says he's from the south of Germany. I go over and hug her because among Mrs. Prescott and my mother and Rena, she's the only hugging type I've seen today, even though she's tall and skinny. The policeman wants a sample of my handwriting. My mother tries to sound protective.

"She doesn't need to give it to you," she says. "We've got a million samples all over the house."

Rena whispers to me that they have checked her handwriting, too. Rena has very girlish writing. In fact, she writes like a fifth-grade girl. Which, if I think about it, is probably what she was when she quit school. I tell them I'll write anything they want if they will tell me what this is all about.

In the manila envelope is one of my father's mother's letters. It's the one I read at my party, but that doesn't mean anything because it was the one on top. Scotch-taped to it is a note. The note says, "Hitler didn't kill your mother. You killed your mother."

I go over to the bottom drawer of the desk. Everyone follows me. I can't believe no one has looked. My mother knows about the letters. I pull the drawer open. Slowly, while my mother explains rapid-fire that this is where the letter came from, that it was in a packet, that she should have thought of this before.

The packet of letters is gone. Well, the letters are gone, but the ribbon is lying on the bottom of the drawer, swirled around. And under it is a scrap of paper. I recognize it. It's torn from the pad we keep by the telephone in the kitchen. In the same handwriting as on the note attached to the letter, it says, "You're not so smart."

From *New Orleans Noir (*later a chapter in *Too Jewish.)*

SECONDHAND SMOKE

They both blame me for killing Woodrow. I tell that to Gloretta, and she says, "Well, Ru, they say when you get a divorce, the one the kids're still living with, that's the one they're meanest to."

Gloretta watches too much television, and I tell her that all the time. You can't phone her before eleven or between three and five, no matter what. Woodrow was pronounced dead during *Live with Regis,* and I didn't dare let her know until after *Rosie O'Donnell.* By which time Woodrow was long on his way to the funeral home. That might not mean much, but it was the last chance anyone had to see him. Woodrow wanted to be cremated, not for any good reason except he was so cheap he thought he was getting away with something.

"Chrissakes," I say, "first of all, I didn't divorce him, I killed him. I mean, they say I killed him. You are getting me totally mixed up here. And second, it's not exactly like they're living in this house, eating my food or anything. They're both forty-some years old. And far as I can tell, they both got the hell out as soon as they'd figured they'd drained every penny out of their daddy and me, no looking back."

"Well, they're mad at you," Gloretta says.

"Shit, they're always made at me. You can't leave your mama unless you're particularly mad at her." Wilson lives in Chicago, well, outside Chicago, in Evanston, where everyone from there that I meet at his house is a professor and knows everything and looks at me like I have three heads. Zib has been in Florida so long I'm surprised she has any skin left.

"Well, if how far they go is any indication, your two *are furious*," says Gloretta.

What Gloretta neglects to tell you is that her two girls live in walking distance of her house, of course on the good side of St. Charles Avenue, and that practically the only time she ever sees one is if she accidentally bumps into one in KB's. Which has become less and less likely these days, since KB's, which sold out to a chain but nobody cares, had the great idea of being at every major corner on St. Charles, which means the only people who shop there anymore are the ones

82

getting off at the streetcar stops, black kids going to Wright Junior High and black maids going to work on Soniat Street, mostly; just about the only white people that go in there these days are the ones on fixed incomes like Gloretta and the tourists who don't know any better or they'd be in Disney World. The parking lots are empty; if you've got a car, you drive someplace cleaner and cheaper, for Lord's sake.

"I don't think those two of yours are exactly brimming over with love and devotion," I say.

"Nobody asked you, Ru."

When Gloretta gets like that, I generally find some reason to get off the phone, though she knows too much about everything I do for that to be easy. I can't tell her the doorbell's ringing because she knows mine's been broken since 1983, and she also knows my phone's in the back of the house where I can't hear anybody knocking. Not that I'd answer, anyway, especially not that I'd get off the phone to do it. All that's been to my door in quite a while is Jehovah's Witnesses, and never white ones, either. I usually know when they're in the neighborhood, because it's not Sunday and they're walking up and down the street with one or two starched-up little black kids, looking so important. So I don't move around in the front of the house until I figure they're off the block. Anyway, one time I tried to tell Gloretta that I didn't feel like talking to her right then, and she hung up on me and didn't talk to me for seven months, I counted. So I say, "I got to go to the john, Gloretta; you want me to bring the phone in the john?" and she knows I've got a long enough cord and little enough shame to do it, and she says, "Go, go, I need to get off anyway," a little huffy, but people don't hurt my feelings like that, and I hang up the phone, and I look at it like Gloretta is sitting right inside it, and I say, "You're too sensitive, you old fool," and I feel pretty terrific.

Lest anyone gets the wrong idea, Wilson and Zib are not accusing me of murder. They're not even coming right out and saying I killed Woodrow. They're not like that: that much they have in common. Neither one has said anything direct since I knocked all the disrespect out of them before they were five, and they get disrespect and straight talk completely mixed up. It gets on my nerves.

What they both did — and I fully believe each one did it without talking to the other because they generally can't stand each other — they both sent me an article from the *Wall Street Journal*. Well, Wilson sent me the front page of the *Wall Street Journal* with the article circled in black marker so I'd see the banner up top and know how educated he is, and Zib just sent me a raggedy clipping of the same article, with part of one sentence set off in yellow, just in case I didn't get the point, SECONDHAND SMOKE LINKED TO DISEASE.

They believe everything they see in print, no matter how stupid it is. First of all, I don't see how I can go through two packs, filter tips but two packs, every day since I was eleven, and never have a sick day in my life, and then Woodrow is supposed to die from a couple of wisps of smoke that already have been through my lungs, thank you very much. And he doesn't even die of lung cancer; he dies of this giant grapefruit in his brain. Woodrow was a man who breathed through his mouth day and night with those big funny bucky teeth that never had a cavity even though they were out in the air all the time.

Anything he took in went straight down his windpipe; it didn't go anywhere near his brain. The way I see it, there are too many colleges with too many science majors, and these colleges are sending out all these picky people who have to think about something brand new or they won't have jobs, and they have to forget about common sense very fast. If you believe everything they say, you might as well lie down and die. I pitched both copies in the trash.

Woodrow died June 12, and it's almost October and he's still sitting in a box in the bottom drawer of my dresser. The house is directly across from the Valence Street Cemetery, and I've lived in it since a year after we got married, and I've always said it'd be very nice if whoever went first was buried there so the other one could get over and visit all the time. For about the past twenty years, there's been this fat colored man and what I guess is his wife tending the graves and walkways and little patches of grass. In summer they get a bunch of lazy boys from the archdiocese who pick up grass clippings and pine needles, but otherwise the two of them take care of the whole place by themselves, and sometimes it's not a pretty sight.

There've been two floods in recent years and both times bones have floated up. I used to walk the dog over there, but after a while I got too nervous about what I was going to see, and I walk him down toward St. Charles Avenue now. He's only a Chihuahua dropping wet rabbit pellets, but it gives me a bit of satisfaction for him to go on those fancy lawns. Anyway, I wouldn't have minded being buried in the Valence Street Cemetery, because Woodrow could have gone over there every day or so and raked the gravel on my grave, but he had better plans for himself. Woodrow had to have himself cremated so he can be put in Arlington.

The man got about as far as Subic Bay and crab lice during the Korean War, but he's had this idea of having a flag draped over a coffin and a twenty-one-gun salute ever since he watched the Kennedy funeral on TV. I don't know how they're going to work this, since the cardboard box he's in you could cover with a handkerchief, but I don't mess with the dead, and I'm going to take the dog over to Gloretta's, water the yard, get myself a plane ticket if I can find all our money, and take Woodrow up to Arlington. I just need to get both of his children to decide when they are not too busy to give their father a funeral. There's something about seeing him wheeled out of the house and then getting this box back a week later that isn't exactly right.

I haven't been inside a church *except* for funerals since Wilson got married the first time. But now I can almost see why people go to church, just so they'll have someplace to go and look at that casket when the time comes and know for sure that somebody in particular has died. For all I know, Woodrow rolled out of here and sent me the box UPS. I certainly haven't looked inside. As tight as Woodrow was, he probably didn't pay to have himself reduced to pure ash. I read in *The Star* about a cut-rate crematorium in California that crammed fifteen bodies in one oven, smashed up the bones with a shot put, then shoveled ashes out of big oil drums with coffee cans: three pounds for a woman, five pounds for a man. There're probably more surprises in that box than you'd find in the Valence Street Cemetery after a hurricane.

I wait until nine o'clock to call Wilson. You'd think that after teaching the same classes for ten years, he'd know his lines by heart, put in his fifteen hours a week lecturing from memory, then go home and relax. Especially when he teaches things like Organic Evolution. I don't know the first thing about Organic Evolution, but I can tell from the name of it that it has nothing to do with fast-breaking news. There are bound to be subjects where finally everything there is to know has been figured out, and Wilson probably teaches half of them. But I can call him up when I assume the rates go down at five, and that girl he's married to now will answer all out of breath and act like I'm crazy to think anyone would be off work at five; she's only home herself because she has this little business set up in the basement of their house so she can ignore her children and pretend she's better than me.

I've said in front of her, "There may be some people worse than me, but nobody's better than me," and I think she gets the idea of where I stand, but she still looks awfully satisfied all the time.

"He's not in yet, Jerusha, but he ought to be," she says.

That's another thing about her that drives me crazy. Wilson's first wife never called me anything, just waited until I was looking straight at her. She'd call me Gammy to her kids, "Give Gammy a kiss." Jesus! But she couldn't settle on what to call me herself until after the divorce, when she took back her maiden name and started calling me Mrs. Bailey, very polite. So when Wilson up and got married again while he was still asking Woodrow for help with his child support, I said to the girl, "Okay, right off, figure what you're going to call me, and then get used to it."

She laughed, not at all nervous I thought, and she said, "So, what are my options?" and I felt like saying, "Well, how about Mrs. Bailey or Mrs. Bailey?" But instead I said, "Well, the first one calls me Mrs. Bailey, and Zib calls me Mama, and Wilson calls me Mother, and my friends call me Ru."

"I don't know my category yet, do I?" she said, as flip as hell I thought, and then she asked me what Ru was for, though a lot of people do, thinking about that little Roo in the cartoons or that actress Rue McClanahan on TV.

I always say, "R-U like in Jerusha," and then I sit back and wait for them to say, "That's a beautiful name. Is it Russian?" Even a couple of ministers never heard of it; I'd get a kick out of trying it out on a Jehovah's Witness one day when I have absolutely nothing else to do. The truth is, I was born two weeks late, and finally my mother said to God, "You get this damn baby out of here, I swear I'll give it a religious name," and then I came out about eight hours later.

My mother said, "Well, no sense pulling a fast one on God," so she got my father to bring her a Bible, which was no small feat considering they didn't have one, and she closed her eyes, still half asleep from the gas, and she let the Bible fall open. Lucky for her, it fell open to the Old Testament, because there are a lot more women in the Old Testament, the New Testament being the story of a bunch of men who generally didn't fool around.

Right in the middle of Second Kings, there was exactly one female, somebody's mother, though that somebody was a king, and that's how I got my name. My father wanted to name me Mildred, so I'm just as happy that's the way things turned out. I am strictly not a Millie type. I am also not a Jerusha type, but Wilson's wife jumped on it as though she'd picked it out herself.

"From the Bible, right? I remember: the missionary's wife in *Hawaii* — you ever read *Hawaii*? Her name was Jerusha, I've always loved that name, we'll probably name one of our daughters after you, oh, this is terrific."

So far they've got one girl and one boy, and they're named Morgan and Connor. No one ever knows which is which, but I guess she's sobered up considerably since she got married. Her name is Barbara, but I don't call her anything. It's sort of a private joke with myself. "So," I say.

"So, you want him to call you when he comes in?"

"So how are things?" I don't feel like letting her off so easily.

"Good, good." I can picture her, looking around that big old farmy kitchen, hoping something will make a huge noise so she'll have to excuse herself. I've been there twice, and the best way to describe that kitchen is that everything teeters. She has sweet-potato vines covering practically half the room from a single jar, pots of thyme and basil that she plucks from, an overhead rack of unscoured pots that bump and rattle and look like they're all going to come crashing down any minute, and wooden toys all over the floor; give one of those kids a plastic toy, and it'll have disappeared the next day. The house has three stories plus a basement, with about three times as many rooms as my house, and everyone sits in that kitchen and waits for huge, disastrous noises, I swear.

Nothing happens, and I sit and wait, smiling.

"Connor is going to start reading any day now," she says finally.

"It's about time," I say. Connor is five and has been in

kindergarten two months now. "Wilson picked up the newspaper and started to read 'Dondi' when he wasn't quite three," I say.

"I know." The woman is proud of her husband except when he's my son. "Regression toward the mean," she says after a while.

"Whatever."

She doesn't say anything, and even though I'm paying for the call, I don't mind waiting. "How've you been?" she says finally, and I think she is stifling a yawn.

"Pretty good," I say, and the suggestion of a yawn makes me launch into a full-sized one. It's so big it's trembly.

"You know, it's only been, what, four months? It's all right to feel bad." I count back, just to be sure she's talking about Woodrow and remembering correctly while she's at it.

"Three and a half months," I say.

"If anything happened to Wilson, I don't think I'd ever get over it," she says.

"Wait 'til you've be married another forty years."

"I imagine it's worse."

"Not really." I'm not in the mood for sympathy, to tell the truth. But I'm not going to tell her that. This is the first she said about Woodrow since he died. Her parents look like they're both in their fifties and have skinny legs and a tan even in winter; they play golf like it matters, and they live in a Chicago suburb so fancy that the household help is all Polish. The girl isn't going to know a whole lot about death for a long time; I'll cut her slack on that.

"Maybe you're still kind of numb," she says, her voice very soft. "I mean, it was so sudden."

"Are you crazy? You call a man lying around screaming in pain for three months sudden? You want time to stretch out forever, you sit in a house and listen to somebody holler for help, like you can do a thing about it, every day, all day, for *three* months. I almost lost my mind. No, honey, I'm not numb."

"Okay, okay."

"Look," I say after a while, "I just called up to tell Wilson one thing, just tell him one thing. Tell him I am getting to be a nervous wreck with that box sitting in my bottom drawer. Tell him to call up that sister of his, pick a date, let me know, and I'll fly Woodrow up there. Okay?"

"Sure," she says, "I understand." And she actually sounds like she does.

I let the dog out onto the front lawn after I hang up. The street is completely quiet. Usually this time of night, bands of grinning colored boys come walking by, hammering on each other with drumsticks and talking to each other in loud, happy, challenging voices. I think it's quite fine when there is a lot of noise in the street, because it means no one is trying to sneak and hide and hurt somebody.

I don't see anyone for three blocks in either direction, and I wish the grass weren't so wet, and the dog weren't taking such a long time sniffing and wiggling his little butt and making false starts and then sniffing again. "Get a move on, Mealworm," I say, loud enough to surprise him and scare myself a little. All that's out here to hear me are the dead people across the street. He drops a few sweet, tiny turds on the grass, and I pick them up with a Kleenex and carry them back inside and flush them down the toilet.

The house is as quiet as the street, and I hear every small sound: the tic-tac of the dog's nails on the wood floor; water dripping from a clogged gutter at the back, even though it hasn't rained since late morning; the refrigerator kicking on so it can cool a half a jar of mayonnaise, two sticks of margarine, and two jars of blackberry jam that Woodrow didn't live long enough to eat. It takes me a hell of a long time to go to sleep, to tell the truth.

Reprinted with permission from *Chapbook, Deep South Writers Conference* (later a chapter in the novel *Secondhand Smoke).*

JUST SO MUCH

I wasn't an asthmatic or allergic or demanding child. I think maybe twice I told my mother that I *needed* a cat, but she felt my father had left her with enough as it was, and she wasn't going to go out and volunteer to take care of anything extra. I was three when my father blew out an aneurysm an hour before the topping off ceremony of a building on Loyola Avenue. Maybe he wouldn't have survived either the fall or the insult to his brain, but even when I was older the subject never came up between my mother and me.

I could step dreamily into the traffic on Canal Street, or press my hands and face up against the glass observation tower atop the Trade Mart, and she would become very pale and whisper, "No accidents, Anna, you better remember that, there are absolutely no accidents," and I would shrug and silently press forward, surviving.

She let me keep a cat when I was seventeen and she had decided I was almost ready to go. The cat showed up one morning, in the window next to the kitchen table that looked out onto the side gallery. He had no more than a three-inch ledge, but at the time he found me he was a rather lithe, busy cat, and he could balance there and wait patiently, not slip off, look longingly at my buttered muffins and cafe au lait, as if he would give up all the emerald lizards in the graveyard if he could just come in, please, and sit on the empty chair at the table and get ready to take my place.

I named him Ansel Adams. Ansel Adams did brilliant things with nothing more than black and white. The cat was, I realized much later, a type, a mostly black cat with white on his belly and splashes of white in arbitrary places, creating no symmetry, but making me look for balance through squinting eyes, an oriental screen sort of cat. After he came into the house and began to grow fat and lazy, I would lie on the floor and study him, curled up, trying to figure out where patterns came from.

"Do you think, Mama, that maybe in the womb there is just so much white to go around, and it spatters around from the walls, so if you could lay the kittens out in the right array, you'd see pictures, white on black?"

"If you are there imagining God with a paintbrush, lying with his back up against some cat's viscera, you're not as

95

ready to leave as I think," she said. "Come here, Ansel Adams, you may be out of a job soon."

Once I was finished with high school and my mother was letting me wait to begin my life, I spent my days at the library on St. Charles Avenue. The library was a mansion donated in memory of a son killed in the war, and most weekday afternoons it was mine, the broad porches and stone steps, the separate garages the size of Mama's house, the manmade hillocks. I'd lie on a patch of grass, oak pollen forming a blanket under me, and read *The Castle* and *The Voyage of the HMS Beagle* when I wasn't just watching. I stayed away from those dusty, jacketless books full of facts that were in the upstairs back stacks and avoided, too, the slick journals full of science that sat on the reading desk in the front room, the ones my mother went over to read page by page on Saturday mornings while I slept.

My mother had never gotten past the fact that, by the time she was twenty-seven, she was the widow of a construction worker, a woman who had no more schooling than it took to decapitate rats for two dollars an hour in the cytology lab at the medical school. I sensed it pleased her that my father's government check let me spend my days slipping out the side door of the library and into my dreams, happy to learn nothing more than that the idle rich have marvelous things to look at all day. She was planning on my becoming one of them.

I married George after a year, and Ansel Adams had his

96

place secure in my mother's house. He grew a fine inguinal pouch with two fat, useless teats under his white belly, and lay around waiting for my mother to say something so he could ignore her. Because my mother said it was time, I became pregnant a respectable two months after my wedding, and George went downtown to work in a law firm in the same building where my father had plummeted to the ground fifteen years before.

The corridors were narrow and needed paint, signs of respectability and dignity in New Orleans, and the sidewalk had been replaced at least twice since my father's death, but George didn't think about much more than going down to that building twelve hours a day so he could be a partner. I didn't know him particularly well, so his long days were fine: I could get by effortlessly, promising him nothing more than that I'd never tell anyone how my father died. It was no crime not to finish high school, I said to him once, and he said, "Well, in my family it *was*."

Days, I sat around Mama's shotgun house and got as fat as Ansel Adams, and since I was not even nineteen years old, the doctor gave me vitamins and pushed his hand up inside me until I yelped in pain; it was not until my eighth month that he noticed I looked frightfully huge and pressed a stethoscope all over my belly for a few minutes and said distractedly, "No doubt about it, you're not big, *they're* big."

"They're?"

"Two of them," he said. "Are you ready for two of them?"

All George said was, "Don't have an ultrasound. I don't want weird pictures on the mantel."

Twins are supposed to come early, but the entire month passed without any sign that they were ready. I could have spent my days at my own house, two solid levels of stucco painted the color of crab fat, with a shell of a New Orleans raised basement and a queer L-shaped pool that wrapped around, side and back. It was a house that George chose because it was a half block off St. Charles Avenue.

"It's unsightly," I said, trying to sound as if I were joking when I saw it the first time, marveling that anyone who had to put a fresh coat of paint on a house to sell it would choose such a color. "With the house in the way, you can't see anyone in the shallow end of the pool if you're in the deep end; what's the fun of that?"

"What counts is the address," George said with the air of someone who's had seven more years of schooling and is entitled to a lot. And you can put your mother in the basement. I shrugged, ashamed to be glad I was pregnant, so soon I wouldn't have to let him touch me.

It was June, and I could have lain out by the pool; I could have floated and pivoted in the pool, weightless even with the water sac that held two babies inside me. I could have lain on a raft, navigating through the sharp right angle where the pool filled the downtown-river corner of our lot. But I spent the days instead at my mother's house, staring at Ansel Adams and half listening to my mother saying good things about George.

"Your father was intelligent, too, same as George," she said. "Probably you'll have two smart babies. They'll build monumental things, they just won't be dumb enough to go standing on top of them in the middle of June until the blood boils in their heads."

My water broke on the anniversary of my father's death, June 21. I was in my mother's kitchen, and the last thing I saw when I left the house was Ansel Adams tiptoeing behind me, licking up the liquid on the floor.

The first baby came, and the doctor said, "A boy, ten twenty-nine," and I lay still on the table, myopic and dazzled, feeling nothing except vague impulses from the waist down, and one minute later the nurse said, "Oh, Jesus oh, Jesus, oh, Jesus," and the doctor said, "Get her the fuck out of here."

A curtain went up over me, extended across the point at my middle where sensation ended, and the nurse who had not been thrown out said, "Honey, you go to sleep now, you're all right, OK?" The funny thing was, I was in a room full of strangers, with George in his office knowing nothing, and my mother somewhere in the hospital pale and full of misgivings from what I could tell when I last saw her, and going to sleep seemed like an excellent option.

"What happened?"

I remember whispering through the sort of sleep that only breaks if I open my eyes. I wakened later to hear my mother saying to George, "The doctor says he thinks it's called mosaic scrambling, maybe there's an error in the DNA, a translocation error."

I heard myself saying, "But what *happened*?" and my mother went on about chromosomal changes not being hereditary, as if she'd never heard me, and I dozed again.

We named the first one George Junior. George Senior did not want to name the second one because he was positive he was going to die. The child had no arms or legs to speak of, just stumps of varying lengths, none reaching as far as a knee or elbow joint, tubes of flesh over bone with smooth, rounded tips. But I loved touching him, learning his bones, his skin as warm and alive as his brother's. I named him Gregor, after Samsa and Mendel; it was almost an anagram of George, an extra R, one less E.

"Gregor, he's the one who'll have imagination," I said to George Senior, who had both eyes on the television set.

"Not even thinking up a new name for a child doesn't give him a lot of options. Poor little George."

My husband wasn't hearing me.

"Poor little Gregor," I said for my own benefit, lying supine in that hospital bed in that private room with no flowers, tears streaming down into my ears. No one knew what to do, congratulate or condole, and so no one did anything, not even the secretarial pool on the third level of

100

George's law firm. People's silence helped George, made him feel once again that he was right and I was wrong.

I cried over Gregor until he was old enough to notice, by which time he had so much spirit in him that I didn't need to do so much crying. I could change George Junior's diaper, and he'd kick at me so hard that it would hurt; he was the sort of boy who would rock back onto his neck when he was two so that when his heels hit my arm simultaneously he'd leave two perfect round bruises side by side; I'd want to smack his leg, angrily, reflexively, disliking him for a fraction of a moment, and he'd smile with pleasure.

Gregor, on the other hand, had no time for mischief, and of course no power for it, either. He was too busy concentrating on figuring out new ways to do things, rolling over through pure will, scooting on the carpet on his stubs until they bled, so my mother began crocheting him tiny heelless red socks with elastic to hold them around his limbs, and after a morning of clumping around the house he would have purple rings on the stumps and a look of triumph on his face that George Junior never had unless he was stealing something. I would be sure to *tell* anyone that they were identical twins.

"I *told* you prostheses were unnecessary," George Senior would say. "*I'm* the Presbyterian here," I'd say back, but George didn't laugh or acquiesce.

Gregor gave up trying to get around when they were both two and George Junior began to run so fast that his head bumped into low tables; George Junior would let out a shrill of pain, look back at Gregor, who was full of simple amazement, and then George Junior would keep running until his feet carried his head straight into another obstacle. Gregor perfected the skill of sitting up straight in a stroller, and his body became thick and wise while his brother ran about, knees covered with skin like that of old reptiles, stitches in three places on his face from three separate trips to the hospital.

George Junior had as little sympathy for Gregor as he did for Ansel Adams, the only difference being that he could torment the cat by chasing him. George Junior would not fetch anything for Gregor. Not that Gregor asked, even from the earliest times in his life, when he had no words, only grunts, sounds that George Junior didn't need to make because he could grab whatever he pleased. George Junior treated him as if he were a beggar at an intersection where his car was stopped; he moved slowly past, not letting his eye be caught, not having to give, not having to feel anything, either.

It was a few weeks after their sixth birthday. My mother had been living with us for some time, hiding in her basement rooms in the evenings when her son-in-law was home, otherwise roaming the house freely. Ansel Adams had no such scruples, no fear of being told to go away. George took a liking to him when he moved in.

"He was probably a terrific litigator in his last life," he said about Ansel Adams. "This is one no-bullshit cat."

"They're all like that," my mother said, missing the point. George had not touched one wall or tool since he bought the house, but he went out one day and bought all the makings for a pet door, and in three Saturdays of skinned knuckles and cursing with tears in his eyes, George installed a swinging trap door at the head of the basement stairs so that Ansel Adams could choose where he wanted to spend his time.

When Ansel Adams came into the bedroom at night and slept on the backs of George's knees, George would come to breakfast complaining in a way that let my mother know he felt he had won her cat away from her. Ansel Adams still had his claws, and George respected him for that.

I was getting ready to go outside by the swimming pool with the two boys that afternoon. It was one of those summer days when a black cloud would stretch all the way from Texas to the Atlantic Ocean, leaving the Deep South awash in rot and sweat while everyone waited for the thunderstorms to break in a band moving west to east, cooling everything off for half an hour before the steam rose again a few hours before sunset.

" It is going to absolutely storm," I said to George Junior. "We have a lightening rod on the top of the house," George Junior said. "Lightning, George, lightning," Gregor said. "Besides, lightning likes water better."

"You want to go out to the pool or not?" George Junior said.

"Well, not if I'm going to get killed," Gregor said, and my mother whispered to me, "You've done a good job."

I gave her a blank look.

"He doesn't want to get killed," she said.

"Oh, I am a terrific mother, all right," I said.

"You're kind of dead anyway," George Junior said. He looked like his father at that moment, and I tried to pretend he was Gregor so I wouldn't hate him.

"Mama!" Gregor said.

"Sorry," George Junior said, not meaning it. "But it's true," he whispered into my mother's ear loudly enough for me and Gregor to hear him. He took the basement steps two at a time, almost tipping Gregor out of my arms, leaving my mother there, squinting into the semidarkness after him.

Gregor had his own special pool raft, cumbersome and safe, an inner tube balanced on three-foot pontoons and rigged inside with straps that kept him upright in the water. Gregor could actually navigate well, though of course there was nothing streamlined about his limbs, no cupped hand or flattened foot that would push water behind him so that he could move quickly. I would race him with my fists outstretched in front of me, using only my legs for propulsion, and it was a fair race, though George Junior would thrash alongside us, face in the water, arms churning, passing, hitting the far end of the pool, taking a breath, coming back and making a circle around us, crashing past us again, often beating both of us on his second pass.

"Well, Mama's the rotten egg," Gregor would say, and George Junior would say, "You're the rotten egg, Gregor," then clamber up onto the side of the pool and belly flop in next to his brother, rocking the raft and sending water up into Gregor's nose.

I watched the clouds over the river for streaks of lightning, but none came, and the clouds didn't move toward us, so I let George Junior into the deep water that ran alongside the house, rigged Gregor up, launched him in the shallow portion at the back of the property. The water was surprisingly cold for the dead of summer, shocking each little fat pocket unpleasantly as I lowered myself into the pool. The sunlight was stronger because it had fought through the cloud cover; not thinking, I put my hand up to shade my face, then lowered it, preferring the warmth.

Elbows up on the edge of the corner of the pool where it turned at the back of the yard, chin thrust upward, feet pedaling gently, protected now from the sun by blooming bougainvillea that hung out over the water and left the pool full of lipstick-pink petals each morning, I didn't even notice George Junior going into the house for a snack, didn't notice him until he came out. Gregor was floating past me.

"Mama, you know Ansel Adams is out here," Gregor called to me after a while.

Ansel Adams stood next to the pool, blinking in disbelief at his good fortune. He had not been outdoors in years, except in a carrying case. George Junior went over to crouch next to him, laid his ice pop on the slate surface; it puddled in the heat. He put his finger to his lips, reached for the cat, lifted him up under the pits of his front legs, most of Ansel Adams's bulk bumping against his knees as George Junior carried him toward the deep arm of the pool.

"No!" I said.

George Junior kept walking, his back arching with the effort of carrying a cat fully one-third his size. He was moving toward the deepest end, where Gregor had drifted.

"I mean it, George," I said. George Junior sat down on the edge of the pool, lowered his feet into the water. Ansel Adams wriggled a little, showing dissatisfaction, but not particularly wanting to escape. And then, cat and all, George Junior jumped into the pool.

It was all too much for Ansel Adams, who perhaps could have managed being gently lowered into water, for all I know. The cat went under with George Junior and while the boy bobbed up fine the first time, the cat came up fighting as if someone had shot him full of amphetamines. He flew into the air, clawing at George Junior, landing on Gregor's raft, catching a claw in the taut rubber, and puncturing it in three places.

I tore through the water as if it gave as little resistance as a vacuum, reached into the fray, pulled back instinctively when Ansel Adams raked me with his teeth, grabbed for him again, and then he sunk his claws into me so deep that I wanted to let him drown.

Both boys and I were in eight feet of water, and now all I could see were the identical faces of my sons, one with his hair dry and soft and almost white in the sun, the other with his hair dark with water, one with a look of pure terror on his face, the other with a look of mild annoyance, as if I'd come along and ruined his perfectly good idea for amusing himself. I caught the cat around the middle, and it slipped through my hands, landing on top of George Junior, covering his face and scratching at his eyes in panic to get a hold.

"Mama!" Gregor said. He was now snared in the straps of a heavy, sinking, tipping vessel, a craft we trusted as long as everything went all right. I tore at the straps, made no headway, began pushing him toward the shallow end; I would have to move him a full twenty yards and around a bend to get him moored at the steps.

I screamed for my mother, my voice echoing in an empty summer neighborhood.

I looked back toward George Junior, and I couldn't see

him or Ansel Adams anymore. I pushed Gregor to the steps. It was all I could do.

Used with permission from *Louisiana Literature* (later a chapter in *Odds)*

JAPANESE PLUM TREE

The two neighboring houses mirrored each another, like left- and right-handed twins, cottages with a shuttered window each, a rail around the porches, gingerbread. Always painted the same color, white into the seventies, then pale yellow, then peach, then mauve. When Margaret and I were small, we noticed that, together, the houses looked like nothing so much as a great, grinning face, with eyes, nostrils, teeth, curls. Margaret's family lived in the house on the left, her grandmother Eleanor in the one on the right, and she and I would sit across the street, on the curb, safe when New Orleans was safe, and give the person that was the houses a life, a name, a make of car, a school.

When we were fifteen, my mother and I dropped Margaret at home after piano lessons. "Symmetry offends the gods," she said to my mother apologetically one afternoon, and we never again thought about the two houses taken as one.

Margaret's great-grandfather designed the houses in 1903. He had a small parcel of land in Faubourg Bouligny, small being the only sized residential lot to be found in New Orleans by an average person. Sixty feet across, enough for two cottages. He planned to move into one with his wife and two children, leave the other vacant, expecting his son Philip, at that time a small boy, to occupy it with his own family when he was grown. Lumber and labor were cheaper when building two houses at once and, he must have reasoned, the old Creole arrangement of putting bachelor quarters behind the main house was foolish, inviting nothing but trouble. He wanted no transitions for his son.

Instead his daughter Eleanor was the first to occupy that house. The great-grandfather died in timely fashion, so Eleanor's son, Margaret's father, had the first house waiting for him when he married. It was a matter of control, Margaret always said. "Who can grow up with his parents next door?" (When she married, though, she forgot her protestations, moved in next to her parents when her grandmother Eleanor died, painted yellow when they said yellow, peach when they said peach, mauve when they said mauve.)

Though they had identical, if reversed, floor plans, the houses were dissimilar inside when we were children: Eleanor had stains, so Margaret's mother had antimacassars; Eleanor fried fish, so Margaret's mother filled the air with the scent of baking chocolate.

"I wonder what your mother'd do if I took up the piano," Eleanor said to Margaret once.

"I play the piano," Margaret said.

"I know," Eleanor said. "Don't worry, I won't."

Margaret's great-grandfather had had a limit on what he could dictate; for him only the exterior had mattered. So landscaping matched, six white azalea bushes, a border of monkey grass, a thicket of banana trees; when the banana trees on one property died in the 1963 New Year's Eve snowfall, Eleanor transplanted half of the survivors from the other side to take their place.

A single difference existed between the exteriors of the two houses. Behind the one on the left grew a Japanese plum tree. Full of fruit in spring and twenty feet tall, the tree was not concealed by the house, but rather was highly visible from the street. I asked Margaret once about the Japanese plum tree. I guess we were under the age of ten, because I took the story seriously enough to stay away from Margaret's house for several months afterwards.

"Oh, Mama wants to cut that tree down," Margaret said. "She says, 'If we're going to be a laughingstock, might as well go all the way.'" I knew what she meant, the mirror houses having become a landmark; tour buses did not pass, but cars with local license plates often came by slowly, with three or four adult passengers looking intensely interested.

"But Nana Eleanor told my mother, 'Don't you dare. You come into this family, you show some respect.'"

We were sitting on the curb opposite her house, splay-legged, trying to roll marbles only halfway across the street, aiming to have them hit the top of the rise in the middle of the blacktop, then come back. We weren't winning or losing from one another, but rather were ignoring our misses, ignoring our successes, too. I liked the wrist action, the laziness of the motion.

"I told Mama, 'One day Nana's going to be dead, and you can chop down the tree,' and she laughed," Margaret said. "My uncle Philip died in that tree, see."

I stopped rolling marbles. I was keenly interested, so Margaret parceled out the story in fragments. Uncle Philip wasn't an uncle at all, at least not the way I might picture an uncle. For one thing, he was a great-uncle. For another, he was only seven years old when he died. In my mind I did what arithmetic I could, changing Uncle Philip from a man in a suit—no, weekend trousers—no, nineteen-forty-something, to a boy in long curls, short pants, in nineteen-ought some-thing. He was Eleanor's brother; I put Margaret's grand-mother in long curls, short skirts. Philip had to pick the top plums.

111

"The nigras come in the yard, put their fingers on the low-hanging ones," he told his sister.

"Coloreds," Eleanor corrected him, disgusted. She went back into the house.

He was supposed to stay away from that tree. It had been on the land when her father bought it, standing within ten feet of two other, more mature Japanese plum trees across the back property line. Can't take him away from his mama and daddy, Eleanor's father had reasoned about the young tree, and when he set out to build his identical houses he picked up plums in spring and planted the smooth brown seeds in a spot in the other yard he had measured to mirror that of the original tree. None grew, and after a while he told his children to ignore the Japanese plum tree, that it was a trespasser.

When Eleanor heard nothing from Philip, she tiptoed out into the yard. In spring, the grass was supple, the few leaves on the ground green and soft, too, and her footfall made no sound. She looked up into the tree. Philip was near the uppermost branches, clinging to one, reaching for another, around his neck a length of rope that he had tied to a higher branch. She asked him what the rope was for.

"So if I fall I won't hurt myself," he said.

It seemed like a good idea to her. Eleanor was six. When Margaret found herself orphaned in her mid-thirties, she decided it was time to move, to keep a rhythm, and she returned to the house on the left. The other stood

112

vacant.

"I'll buy it. Or rent it," I told her.

"Rent with the option to buy," she said, unable to make up her mind.

She and I had a certain symmetry: no husbands, children six and seven, hers both girls, mine both boys. The first night we moved in, with no beds up on frames, everything in boxes, power and water off, the boys were to sleep in the room with me, on piles of quilts, beaming flashlights at each another in the dark, checking.

At midnight, when it was clear that none of us was going to doze off soon, I told them the story of Uncle Philip.

"Eleanor didn't tell anyone he was hanging until it was too late," I said. "She thought he knew what he was doing."

"People used to be really stupid," John-Ryan said. "I'm going up in that tree tomorrow."

"*I'm* going to sleep with Mama," Peter said, though he already was lined up alongside me, his little stick of a body bending this way and that to conform to my contours.

"Your little brother has a lot more sense than you do," I told John-Ryan. "If you want Japanese plums, you use a ladder."

In the dim beam of an overused flashlight, I saw annoyance on his face, and he dragged his covers into the next room, leaving us and the light. When I went in at daybreak, he was deep asleep in the corner of the room, his behind tucked neatly into the angle where the walls met, his fists tight. He didn't awaken until almost eleven, heard none of the sliding of heavy cardboard containers on the floor, none of Peter's exclamations over toys he found at the bottom of boxes, toys Peter had played with two days before. From time to time I checked John-Ryan's breathing; it was slow and even. He slept that way after long days at the beach, his body drained of salt and muscles stretched to their limits; after a while I reasoned that the move might have had the same effect on him, and I let Peter push me out into the backyard, peering around me.

"I don't see a dead boy," he said, looking up into the lower branches of the Japanese plum tree.

John-Ryan had shambled out, squinting in the sunshine.

"He's at the top," he said.

Peter looked up quickly.

"The boy's been dead almost a hundred years," I said.

"So?" Peter said.

"I was joking, stupid," John-Ryan said. "This is a lousy house."

He turned to go inside, his pupils pinpoints, his arms folded across his chest. Peter let out a wail, keen with insult or disappointment; I couldn't tell. John-Ryan had given Peter expectations of kindness: he was the sort of boy who put his empty pistachio shells by anthills, for food, for beds. Since infancy, John-Ryan had never fretted, except when he was short of sleep. A night at a friend's house, of boys betting who'd be the last to see the clock, was inevitably followed by a fussiness that took days to fix.

"You slept all day; what's your problem?" I said, having trailed him into the still-dark house. NOPSI had not come to turn on the power; the ceilings were remarkably low for an old house. Margaret's great-grandfather had ignored much for the sake of the horizontal.

"I did guard duty," he said, not miserably, not arrogantly, just matter-of-factly. I pulled him to me, the top of his head knocking my chin. He had lived in a house with his father long enough to have vague ideas about the posturing men did.

"We'll have lights tonight," I said. John-Ryan's muscles didn't loosen; his body didn't mold to mine.

"I'm too old for lights," he said.

It was early April. The Japanese plum tree was full of yellow fruit. Margaret brought her girls and a ladder over that evening; the yards were undivided, the grass cut at the same time, and I imagined us there in ten years, the sexual tensions between her children and mine grown ugly with no barriers. Her older girl clambered up the ladder, disappeared into the lower branches, and began tossing plums, plucking off fistfuls so some of the fruit rained down mashed and bruised. "Mama!" said the other, examining a single plum turning to a mealy paste in her hand. Peter was filling a paper grocery bag with her rejects, as if they were cheap plastic beads at a Mardi Gras parade: what counted was the heaviness of his sack.

"I do *not* have to let you stay up there," Margaret said to the one in the tree.

The Nashes were in their yard. They had owned the property behind the mirror houses since before I knew Margaret. A black couple with no children, so grown in on each other that they'd have to die at the same time. They had cut down the two Japanese plum trees in their yard decades ago, giving no reason, putting out strawberry beds in the unblocked sunlight. They would pass a colander of berries over the fence each May, and no child, black or white, ever had trespassed onto their property.

"A child in a tree a bad idea, you know that well as me," Mrs. Nash said to Margaret. "You don't see nobody falling out no strawberry patch."

"I'm watching her," Margaret said. "You might be watching her kill herself," Mrs. Nash said, and her husband nodded in agreement. They stationed themselves at the fence, ready to scurry off for help.

I looked at John-Ryan, who stood at a distance from all of us, the way he skirted live oaks in buckmoth caterpillar season. "You don't have to climb," I whispered to him.

"I'm not climbing with a girl, that's all," he said low, so only Peter and I heard him. Peter edged away from the tree, reluctant, but loyal.

"You want to take turns?" I spoke in a normal tone so Margaret could hear; I'd need her cooperation. John-Ryan shook his head vigorously, no, and Margaret gave me the sort of indulgent smile one might expect from the mother of a winner.

"Aw, come on, he could if he wanted to," I said, and I tried to see her girls through a young boy's eyes, their fuzzy calves, their scabby brush burns, their sweet cheesy scent. Margaret's girls did not look promising; only the fact that Margaret had filled out with hips and a thick head of hair gave me enough imagination to have hope for them. John-Ryan had no such point of reference. Margaret had known me too long: "Hey, we don't like *them*, either," she said.

We had beds and lights--and not much else--that night, but John-Ryan insisted on sleeping where he slept the night before. He sat on top of a pile of quilts, propped himself in the corner, a small portable television on the floor between his legs. He plugged the set in, but didn't turn it on.

"Security guards watch TV," I said when I passed through the room on the way to bed.

"They're just getting paid; I'm serious," he said. I heard a tremor in his voice, so I offered to sleep nearby. He shook his head, no. "She doesn't tell parents anything," he said. She? "My friend." My eyes registered surprise. "If you tell Margaret I'm friends with a girl, I'll throw up," he said.

"One of her girls?"

He shook his head, no.

117

"Okay," I said.

For two weeks John-Ryan was moody and nocturnal. Twice his teacher sent him home midmorning, convinced he was feverish. "They don't fall asleep in the morning unless they're sick," she said apologetically. "After lunch, yes, I might even doze off myself."

I cocked my head; the school year was almost out, and I imagined a roomful of second-graders running around endangering themselves every afternoon while their narcoleptic teacher snoozed at her desk.

"But I *don't*," she said. I considered telling her that John-Ryan stayed up nights, talking to an imaginary girl, protecting her, or perhaps protecting me. But I was too tired for explanations.

On a Saturday morning, two weeks after we had moved into the house, I found John-Ryan in his own bed. "I don't need to do guard duty now," he said, awake by seven.

"This is a good house," I said, and he shot me a give-me-a-break grin.

A year to the day after we moved in, the boys' father moved to Baltimore, and John-Ryan began his vigils again. While Peter walked around declaring his hatred for his father, then for me, John-Ryan said to his brother, "Ease up, man. Now you get to go on a plane, and you even get to go in the cockpit. You never saw Dad anyway, big deal," and he built his nest in the living room.

Settled in now, we had pantries and drawers where John-Ryan could find what he needed, so he stashed chocolate *and* D batteries, a rosary *and* sharp scissors, under his pile of bedding. This time I wrote a note to his teacher, full of psychology, telling her to let him put his head down on his desk. I was not doing anything with my days except filling the rooms of my house with plants, herbs and bulbs and vines, seedlings and shoots. I wanted vegetables, but when I told Margaret, she said no. She was superstitious. If I put in bell peppers and mirlitons on my side of the yard, I would have to be damn sure the same came up on her side, and frankly she wasn't in the mood.

So I nursed up bean plants and garlic in my kitchen, and though the plants took a lot of time, I could have fetched John-Ryan from school. I simply didn't want to; I wanted him shamed back to being himself.

The screams awakened me at three in the morning. Peter was tearing through the house, trying to hop into short pants while still in long pajamas, and John-Ryan was running behind him.

"You're having a nightmare, wake up," he called behind his brother.

"No, I'm not," Peter said hotly. He was still balancing on one foot, tangled in his pants. He fell over in a soft heap, began crying noisily. I told him he could sleep in my bed. "That won't help," he said. I stroked his head; his hair was as

119

wet as if he'd been swimming. He looked me straight in the eye. "I'm not supposed to talk to strangers," he said.

"Strangers don't talk to boys when they're with their mothers," I said, and that made enough sense to Peter.

After Peter fell asleep, his brother walked into my room as if he were expected. "We're not supposed to be living in this house," John-Ryan said.

"Oh?" I flicked the bedside lamp on, and he held his palms out, shielding himself from the light. I turned it off, relied on filtered streetlight. John-Ryan sat on the foot of the bed, like a doctor visiting a patient.

"Eleanor doesn't like boys."

"Eleanor?"

"This is her house."

"When I was your age, there was an Eleanor in this house. And she was about a hundred years old, and she liked boys." I didn't know whether that was true, because I had never seen Eleanor around boys, but she had a son, Margaret's father, and liked him well enough to let him live out his life in one or the other of the mirror houses.

"She hates boys," John-Ryan said emphatically.

"Sh-h-h-h." Peter was like someone under anaesthetic, who might have been hearing everything.

John-Ryan shrugged. "Know why I didn't tell you? Because you'd think it was stupid." He stumbled in the semi-darkness toward the door, then stopped. "Maybe I ought to stay in here," he said. I told him that was fine with me.

"Nah," he said, "I might fall to sleep."

Peter was not in the bed when I awakened at first light. I tiptoed through the living room, found my sentry seated at his post, head against the wall, lips pursed in deep sleep. I whispered Peter's name from room to room, tried closets, tried the front door, still dead-bolted. The backyard door was slightly ajar, and I stepped out into the wet cool of an April morning, expecting Peter on his three-wheeler, grinding through the thick grass.

Through the tree branches I saw the bottoms of his Keds, smooth eraser rubber rimmed in white. Stick legs, loose and bearing no weight, disappeared into the wide tunnels of short pants. I closed my eyes and screamed. And screamed. And did not open my eyes, not when the Nashes came into the yard, not when Margaret came out, not even when I heard John-Ryan's screams.

***

Mrs. Nash was puttering around in my kitchen. Food that people had brought had hardened and softened, beef with green patina, pudding oozing water. John-Ryan did not eat, nor did I, and Mrs. Nash had chosen for herself the chore of restoring my refrigerator to normalcy, now that no one else felt obligations to do for me. Three weeks. In three weeks Peter's death was over with for everyone but us. "Not a thing you can freeze," Mrs. Nash said with regret, and I heard the whump of an uneaten casserole hitting the bottom of the

121

garbage can. Mrs. Nash did not have a disposal, didn't expect that I had one, either. I sat at the table and watched her, unhelpful as the inert are privileged to be.

"Trouble is, Margaret think it's one big joke. Well, not no more, but she should of told you. Her grandma been in the 'sane asylum, and Margaret know it, too."

I stared at her. Following her movements was soothing and easy, uncover the bowl, dump it, wipe out what's stuck, drop into soapy water. I couldn't follow her talk at all, certainly found no peace in it, though she had a deep, smoke-graveled voice.

"Eleanor?"

"*Miss* Eleanor, don't think nobody ever call her plain Eleanor, not white, not colored. When Margaret daddy seven, they put that woman in DePaul Hospital. That's when Nash cut down the trees."

She was washing a pie pan, not missing one square inch, working around the 360. Twice, three times.

"When he grown, he have a girl, Margaret, I say, "Thank you, Jesus, then Margaret have two girls, I say, 'Jesus, you know what you doing. You come with two boys, I say, 'Margaret, you out your mind? Margaret say she superstitious, I say to her, 'You count the grasses in them two yards, you think you doing something, but you not. Miss Eleanor pure evil. You don't get rid of pure evil like that."

I began to tremble with the strange relief that comes of

having someone to blame. "She *tell* her brother Philip jump. Don't let nobody tell you no different."

Reprinted with permission from *Louisiana Literature,* Patty Friedmann, guest editor.

HAIRCUT

Selly was my fourth. By the time she came along, and surely by then she came of her own free will, I'd run out of names. I'd used my own, my husband's, and my doctor's, whose mother had been kind enough to call him James, as if she knew she was going to be responsible for many other women's choices.

My young James took one look at the infant, said, "What a selly little baby," and a few months later, when I was in the mood, I went down to the registrar of births and gave her the name.

By the time Selly was six months old, I knew she was my ultraviolet one, and I stopped having children. With each subsequent child, we leached pigment, dried up on volatility.

In early photos they cover a spectrum, light to dark, eyes averted to direct pumpkin-toothed smile. The other three seem a wash; Selly is luminous.

Fourth children are starting-over children, and that is what keeps them from being tiresome, gives them chances. Selly had no successor at the breast, so she stayed at it for three years. And Selly learned to straighten after herself, showing up the other children, so I didn't need to put her out of the house when she was three, left to small-featured, high-voiced nursery women. Selly stayed with me, watching, listening; adults in public places didn't pinch and pluck at her.

"I think she's judging me," they would say.

"Oh, no, she's very happy," I'd say back.

The woman met us at the kindergarten gate. I thought she was the teacher, and my heart sank. Colorless, tan hair, well washed yellow summer shift, sandals that bared unpainted toenails, cracked heels. I smiled at her. "And who's this?" she said, cupping Selly's chin. Selly gave her name, tolerantly, as if for the first time she were judging. The woman smiled with the bottom half of her face. "And what kind of name is that?" Selly up to then had met few people who didn't already know her. "My brother's name," Selly said, and the woman looked at me.

I said nothing.

"*My* daughter's name is Victoria. She's five, too. I assume you're five." *Assyume.* Selly was well nursed, loved

125

by her father, playing catch-up with brothers and sister; she was as big as she could be. "Well, I will be six," she said.

Mrs. Laborde was her name, and she was not a teacher, but rather a mother, one whose idea was not so much to nurture Victoria as to protect her boundaries. She was at the school gate each morning, long after Victoria had gone in, hung up her things, and retreated to the edge of the playground to watch, shrugging when other girls approached her, still watching weeks later after they gave up on her. Mrs. Laborde was in the school room when I brought Selly's cakes for her birthday.

"Is she always here?" I whispered to Selly when I handed her a baking sheet of cakes to pass around the room.

"Who?"

"Mrs. Laborde."

"Sure," she said, as if Mrs. Laborde's presence were more natural than Victoria's.

It was a warm November morning when the school secretary called. "You have to come get Selly, I'm afraid." My first thought was not of injury, but of play gone wrong. Selly had become a magnetic sort of girl, finally larger than everyone else in her days, and she took her power easily, walking sturdily through the halls, dark hair swinging, gathering more little girls around herself than a pretty schoolteacher. I was afraid that eventually she would prove too much for someone. I asked the secretary if Selly was in some trouble. She paused just long enough for me to sense she was the literal type.

"Well, it's head lice," she said.

I laughed, heard silence through the phone. "I have three older children," I said, reminding her of why I took nothing seriously.

"Well, I'd better send for them," she said, missing the point.

Only Selly was guilty, as far as the school could tell, though her brothers and sister did not have telltale cat-black hair. I shampooed them all, a rainbow of hair, darkened by the water, poisons on their small heads, never rinsed enough to satisfy me. A nit comb came with each shampoo bottle, and I put the combs in a drawer, instead used my fingernails to run down each shaft of Selly's squeaky dark hair, going after every mote until I dreamed of them at night, translating the tiny pale eggs into buckmoth pupae in live oaks on the avenues, never eradicated, blocked by foil on trunks, dropping on passersby, exploding under feet, making a city full of people very angry.

"She still has them," Mrs. Laborde said at the school gate the next morning, quite free to tell Selly to bend over, bare the nape of her neck. Selly felt no shame; "Only rich kids get lice," James had told her the night before. "Don't tell her that," I said to James, as I saw Selly's face getting ready to argue her way out of a shampooing with all the gentle effectiveness of a southern lawyer. "But they itch you practically to death," James said helpfully.

I looked quickly where Mrs. Laborde pointed, as blood rushed to Selly's overturned head, saw a white flake or two, nothing eggish, took Selly's shoulder to set her upright. I told Mrs. Laborde I didn't see anything.

"I'm a nurse," she said. Oh? "Yes," she said, as if that explained it all.

The school secretary was already weary of the year, having realized in November that she never was going to have a day without fussing.

"You'll have to do it again," she said when I told her that frankly I didn't see what Mrs. Laborde was talking about. But, I said. "At least you don't have to use kerosene anymore," she said.

I did *not* have head lice as a child, I told her.

I used a full bottle of shampoo this time, hoping pyrethrins came from chrysanthemums, that homecoming queens were taking in as many toxins as Selly, that homecoming queens all lived long enough to look back wistfully, and Selly would, too. I left it on five minutes extra. "You probably got it, too," Selly said when she emerged from the bathroom, saw the sympathetic faces.

"I didn't say nothing," James said.

"Anything," Selly said.

She spent the evening in her room, refusing dinner, accepting two Snickers bars from her father. The other three

128

seemed aimless that night, having spent a good portion of their lives coping with the challenges of Selly, first her newness, then her quiet grabbiness, lately her strange ideas of how to pass time in wise make-believe; no flat-out princesses for Selly when she could be goddess of the moon.

"You'll stay home from school tomorrow," I told her.

James began scratching his head vigorously, and Selly gave him a good fist to the stomach. "Hey," he said, because she never had done that before.

My phone was ringing when I returned home two days later from dropping the children at school with a long detour to the grocery store, a deliberate act. "Come get her," the school secretary said. I took the shampoo and comb with me, a towel slung over my shoulder. I believed the secretary, the way I believed most people who spoke emphatically. Often I went long distances believing such people, politicians and professors, my mother, and I never quite figured out how to question. Mrs. Laborde was in the school office, pacing a broad perimeter around Selly, who sat forward on a plastic contour chair, hands folded, head erect, feet as close to the floor as she could manage. "Don't lean back," Mrs. Laborde was saying. I didn't question her, just held the shampoo bottle up to her as if daring her to come closer. "I'll do it here with witnesses," I said, and Selly shrieked with rage.

"You better take her home," Mrs. Laborde said.

I shook my head, no. The secretary shook her head, yes, and Selly stopped shrieking.

"You may have to shave her head," Mrs. Laborde said, and Selly began to whimper. I took her home.

When I look back, I like to think that it was chemicals that seeped into Selly's brain, because that means one day an antidote will be discovered, not by scientists, but by Selly, who will think about herself and decide her mind needs gentling, the way anxious people now wash the neural pathways with serotonin and quit caring. It wasn't that Selly lost complacency; rather, she added what I imagine was a new lobe in her mind, a pocket of mischief that she found pleasurable when no one else did. She would waken in the night, slip into our bed, run one soft, sweet finger back and forth in an irregular pattern along my arm until I was raw with annoyance. She dropped water into the holes of all the smooth stones in James's collection, packed them in a pound-butter box, stuck it into the freezer, alternately defended herself by saying she forgot or she thought it was a good idea. Over and over she combed the cat, leaving coarse fur puffs on furniture.

"You are making my child insane," I told the school principal the final time I was called in.

"You're going to have to cut it," she said back. She was a sister of the Order of the Blessed Mother, a woman who spoke authoritatively because she never questioned, not the Church, not Mrs. Laborde. Her hair was chin-length, thin and stick straight, as if she had given up the wimple but still needed a modest curtain over the sensuous flesh of her ears. I told her

130

those were Selly's baby curls, never cut; she had no babies to follow her, no need to be easy to tend.

"She's a little young to care what she looks like," the principal said.

Selly wore her sister's hand-me-down school uniform, white blouse, jumper of red, white, and blue plaid. I liked being able to drive up to the school, see the drama of her above the rest.

We went straight to Supercuts, thumbed through magazines looking for women with original genes and makeup that could make even a shaven head one's least salient feature. Selly was not easily fooled. "Their hair is all the same," she said. I pointed out planes and angles, layers and focuses, knowing as little about the patterns of haircutting as I did of underwater channel maps and slopes of mountains. "Mrs. Laborde will be glad no matter what," Selly said hotly, closing the magazine.

"I'll get mine cut first," I said, and Selly brightened considerably.

I told the cutter Selly wanted to be like me; I did not want her to ask why we were taking off twelve healthy inches, for Selly would have told the truth, and the woman would have stopped halfway around her head, tossed us out. Cutters always fussed over their scissors, as if each would lose all she knew if her scissors were used on paper, or wielded by a left-hander, or coated with oils and parasites. It was midday, weekday, slow time, and two cutters circled the chair, sweeping up hair as it fell, looking busy, removing evidence. When we emerged from the shop with identical caps of shiny hair, two colors, like smooth scoops of ice cream on cones, I sighed with relief.

"You have everybody else's hair in a' envelope," Selly said out on the sidewalk.

"You should've said that before," I said.

"No, you should've," she said.

I apologized.

"She still has them, but that's all right," Mrs. Laborde said at the school gate Monday morning. I ignored her. Selly did not have them; I had taken James to the doctor Saturday morning for a throat culture, Selly in tow. The doctor had not noticed the haircut, I suppose because with children one works from charts, not faces, not bodies, which offer few constants.

"I got a haircut," Selly told him as James gagged on the swab. "I got head lice."

"That's ridiculous," the doctor said, passing the culture to his nurse with one hand, running his other hand over the back of Selly's head, tipping it to the light. "You *had* head lice maybe a month ago," he said to her. "What'd you cut her hair off for?" he said to me. Selly took in a gulp of air and regret.

"A nurse told me to."

"In my office?"

I shook my head, no.

"Someone should jerk her license," he said and left the examining room.

***

Over the next two weeks, the dolls in the housekeeping corner of Selly's classroom lost their hair, one by one. "I'm saying nothing," the teacher told me. "To tell you the truth, they needed it." And in fact they were much improved, gnarls and knots removed, leaving only topiary fuzz of odd designs on their flat heads, tempting boys to take a look. Then the girls in the classroom came back shorn, sleek, one by one, until only Veronica was left with enough hair to pin a bow on, shoulder-blade length, thin colorless strands; in the crowd she looked like an old woman who thought she was proving something by wearing short skirts.

Daily now, Mrs. Laborde smiled indulgently at each girl as she passed through the morning gate, as if she were Mrs. Kennedy at the private nursery she'd set up for Caroline in the White House. And eventually Selly came home one day and said, "Veronica hates everybody. And everybody hates her back. And I might go to her house."

"No," I said, "anything but that."

YOU'VE GONE
FROM ME

"It's not as if I'm naming them Adolf and Benito," my mother said.

I've heard this story too many times. Rarely in private where it won't annoy us.

"You can do that, I think," Gammy said. "I think they only call the authorities when you call them Adolf *Hitler* Jones and Benito *Mussolini* Jones. You want me to call the authorities?"

They were in the delivery room. We were the only babies these women had a chance for loving. We were identical *girls*. No Adolf, no Benito. My mother had named us Tragedy and Comedy. Tragedy was mellifluous, and Comedy was perky, she had said. I often wondered which I would have chosen if I'd been given the chance. Mellifluous was not a way to *be*.

134

My mother brought the discussion to an end when my grandmother started thinking about the nicknames we were sure to endure. Trash. Commie.

"You're one to talk, naming me Sibyl," my mother said. "No one knows how to spell it, if the *I* comes first or the *Y*. Not to mention what it connotes."

Gammy told her to work on her birthright of prescience. They always were good-natured with each other. My sister and I knew that pretty much from the start.

***

I was the left-handed one. We mirrored each other, but until we were thirteen, that was our only difference. We didn't even part our hair, just let it fall from the middle. We didn't let friends get close enough to be able to tell us apart, and the only way to tell us apart was how we lived with our names. Unless we used our hands. Those were the ways our mother could tell us apart—that and her insistence on choosing our clothes on days when she might have to call out to us from a distance, generally when we were younger and playing in the park. Gammy began to get older. She managed to look us both in the eye at the same time. "You can't trick me," she would say. "I saw you the minute you were born."

My sister would say, "You're not somebody we'd want to trick," and Gammy would say, "That's how I know you're my Com."

"*She* should be the one to say that," my sister would say, tipping her head just slightly in my direction.

"They got you mixed up in the hospital," Gammy said.

135

Everything changed that year.

***

The day had been regular, with us in power, two against anything anyone would try to pull. The school long ago had quit trying that cute psychological trick of splitting us up so we'd learn something we didn't need. It hadn't worked in the lower grades, when each of us, with no cue from the other, quietly had protested.

"I don't see any reason why I can't be with my sister," I would say. "It's not going to make me like anybody." I would sulk until Comedy was transferred, having said to her teacher, "I don't do work if Tragedy isn't sitting next to me. On my left side, you know."

The school never let her get more than a week behind. I would sit on the left, just as we sat in the booth in the Chinese restaurant, never bumping elbows, and the teacher knew us by place.

That day we were in eighth grade in English, and the teacher thought she was cute, giving us the vocabulary word *redundant* and looking straight at me and my sister. No one in he room except the two of us knew what the word meant.

As I said, it was a regular day. Comedy raised her hand.

"We learned that word in our house," she said. "Because we're *not*."

The teacher smiled with her now-less-cute self. "Does anybody know what she means?"

136

The room was silent. I raised my hand. "Don't you think a roomful of people who don't know something are more redundant than two people who may look like a repetition but have extra things to say?"

My sister whispered to me to hush.

"Sorry," I said.

"Okay, "I said. "All I'll say is that sometimes two things that look alike are different, so don't just throw one out."

This was before kids hid iPhones in their laps. A boy named Jack raised his hand. Everyone could see he was reading from a dictionary shoved halfway inside his desk — everyone but the teacher. "It means 'characterized by verbosity or unnecessary repetition,'" he said.

The teacher smiled as if she'd redeemed herself. "Well, we'll let verbosity go," she said. "I was just playing with unnecessary repetition. And I really wasn't being fair to the twins. I apologize."

We shrugged. "We want some kinds of being redundant," I said. My sister nodded.

It was a regular day.

Until we went to the doctor for our checkup.

Gammy took us. Gammy was the father we never had. She lived with us so our mother could work. The man who donated the power-sperm never came up in conversation much except in a scientific way, mostly when we talked about cell division. If I thought about him at all, I tried to imagine his presence, and I decided it would be too much.

Gammy saw no reason to stop taking two girls who were getting periods and real breasts to a pediatrician. We went after school, so we weren't the only patients who were oversized for the waiting room filled with germy large toys and copies of *Parent* magazine. We had nothing to do. We couldn't even talk to each other because Gammy would want to talk, too. We sat and stared. Some mothers tried not to stare at us. Some little children looked at us, looked again, decided we weren't all that interesting, went back to the Duplo table.

"You know I have a mnemonic," Dr. Mason said when we both were up on the examining table. He'd looked at my chart, pointed at me. "You're Tragedy."

"What's a mnemonic?" my sister said.

"I have a way to remember," he said.

"We're exactly alike," I said. I was thrilled.

"But you put yourselves on the shelf."

"Oh!"

Right then I loved Dr. Mason. Who else knew I always sat on the left?

My love for Dr. Mason didn't last long. He had us undress, and he examined us as only the best diagnostician could, and when we were dressed again, he had us come into his office with Gammy. She would have to tell our mother.

"Have you noticed Comedy struggles a little when she walks?" he said. "I'm not talking about anything frightening. I'm just talking about skeletal issues."

"I think maybe one leg is a little longer than the other," my sister said. "Have you noticed how yours is, too?" she said to me.

"Honey, you have scoliosis," Dr. Mason said to her. "Just you. No accounting for it."

"What the hell is that?" Gammy said. She wasn't being mean. She was just being scared.

He explained that Comedy had a curvature of her spine, but possibly she could stop it from getting worse if she did exercises, though maybe she'd want surgery; it was something he'd need to talk to my mother about.

All I heard was that we weren't the same anymore.

"She's got to have that surgery," I said.

"Hey, speak for yourself," Comedy said.

"What if we're different?"

"What if I die?"

***

Gammy was the only person I thought I could tell about my sadness in the weeks before my wedding. She was going to be one of those grandmothers who waltzed down the aisle on the arm of a man in his twenties, her hair in contemporary style, her seventy-eight years visible only in the shining silver of her hair. I couldn't tell Comedy anything. It had been over a matter of months when we were thirteen that we had lost our perfect symmetry. "Symmetry offends the gods," a girl named Esme said somewhere around then, not in relation to us, but in relation to art, and I had become friends with her.

Esme wasn't going to be my maid of honor because that was wrong, but she would have been otherwise.

"You need to blame your mother, not your sister," Gammy said.

"What?"

We were sitting across from each other at the coffee shop, each with a soy latte, each with three packets of raw sugar. I'd invited her out; we had to go out to talk. That's the way I'd put it.

"You didn't ask me here to talk seating arrangements," she said, and I smiled. I wasn't the sort of bride who cared about the kinds of details that took an entire year to put into place. I'd aimed for fall because I liked the weather, and it gave me six months, so I used six months and had time left over.

"This isn't exactly a time to be sad," she said, "and you're sadder than usual."

I didn't say anything. I didn't need to say anything.

"You sure you want to have this conversation now?"

I nodded. I didn't know much, but I figured that going into marriage feeling sad wasn't quite right. I knew it had to do with Comedy. And that was strange, since she and I hadn't been redundant since eighth grade. At first no one had noticed—no one, that is, except me. And probably Comedy. Our mother certainly hadn't noticed. Now I was three inches taller, I had come back from Northwestern in love and undistinguished, and Comedy had come back from there painfully shy, with grades good enough for law school, a hopeless combination. We had gone to that school because my mother had said they had a drama department and would understand her reasoning. Too many of our teachers along the way had not known the Greek origins of her name choices.

"If I say that you need to blame your mother and not your sister, do you know what I mean?" Gammy said.

"I'm sad. I don't think I should be sad."

"You've been sad since a particular thing happened more than ten years ago," Gammy said. "You want to talk about it?"

"No!" Having a wise person watching me all my life wasn't fair.

Gammy drank her coffee, like a detective on TV. I knew that good cop tactic. I wasn't going to fall for it.

"Comedy was scared of getting surgery, but your mother was more scared," she said. "You absolutely wanted it. You remember that?"

I nodded. Of course. Two against one for the first time.

"Your sister was supposed to do exercises and go swimming. Did she?"

"I tried to make her," I said. I'd even said I'd do it all with her. But the truth was that my mother didn't make her do it.

"You didn't make her do it, either," I said.

"I tried as hard as you did," Gammy said. "Your mother and Comedy just thought it was no big deal. Ignore it, and it'll go away."

I started to feel tears of loss coming on me. They weren't exactly of grief, but more like what I'd expect if someone told me I was going to die soon.

***

A few months after the wedding Gammy gave me a gift only I would understand absolutely. Oh, she also gave the same gift to my mother and to Comedy, and in doing so gave my gift an extra meaning, but maybe only to me. It was a framed photograph that she had arranged so casually that I never noticed anything besides the peskiness of it. Gammy had given me and each of my four attendants identical white slips, and while we were in the dressing room in our white slips making ourselves look dramatic, Gammy had come in with the photographer. I should have suspected something when she hired a woman; probably she would not have done that with a man.

Comedy and I were side by side in front of a very flattering large mirror, putting on the same makeup, putting the same barely perceptible waves in our hair. Dr. Mason's news twelve years ago had not changed what we called "our demeanor," and on this most public day, we were keeping it up. The photographer shot from over my shoulder, catching the backs of our heads and our faces and throats and breasts in our slips in the mirror. I knew what Gammy was telling me. Comedy and our mother hadn't heard about the

142

conversation in the coffee shop, so they didn't know. I certainly had not gone to either one and said, "Well, all this time I thought it was *Comedy's* choice to let herself quit looking exactly like me."

Comedy disappeared during the reception, and no one noticed until the time came for me to throw the bridal bouquet. With so many people in the hall, a search did not take long to find her. She was on the floor of the coat closet that was in little use at that time of the year. She had taken her full bottle of neurontin, a drug she took in far too high a dose because of her pain. What had been a straight line from neck to coccyx when she was thirteen was now a sideways U between those two points. Every step hurt. Every pill helped. Every pill also took her away from what was real. She was up to three thousand milligrams. That day she took ten times that much. She lived, and my wedding reception didn't end until everyone in the room knew she had made it to the hospital and drunk charcoal and been thoroughly saved, except from herself. I didn't go on my wedding trip. I stayed with her eight hours a day and said, over and over, "I wanted us to be the same. Mama didn't care. I should have blamed Mama. I just wanted us to be the same."

"So what now?" she would say in a whisper.

"Something, I'm sure," I would say.

"I don't need to be the same."

"I wanted us to be the same. *Wanted.*"

When Gammy's gift arrived many weeks later, I didn't

explain it to Comedy. I definitely explained it to my husband. He had a right to know, having not hesitated about canceling our trip. He and I had had many talks about why he loved me in particular. I knew without question that if it ever came to needing to let Comedy live with us, I would have no fear that he would cheat with her.

I put the photo on my dresser. I couldn't exactly put it in the living room. Though my mother got a black and white print and put it on her mantel. I never found out what Comedy did with hers.

***

Gammy made the decision. Not my mother, not me, not my husband, not even my sister. I was terribly comfortable in going along with whatever she said we should do. I wondered whether wisdom came with age or whether Gammy always had had more. We were going to be two separate households, and Comedy was going to be part of theirs, hers and my mother's, just as she had been growing up. "This isn't a matter of trust," Gammy had said when she made her announcement in the Chinese restaurant where we used to fit into a booth, me on the left, Comedy on the right. "This is a matter of your being with people who won't make you feel despair," she said to Comedy, who was seated to her right.

"So, we're going to have a lighthearted family meal," Comedy said.

"Touché," my sweet husband said. He had learned quickly how to navigate this world of women. He knew without telling me that he scared them all a little with their unfamiliarity with men up close.

He and I were not going to announce my pregnancy that evening. It wasn't going to make anyone honestly, deep-down happy, except Gammy, and I wasn't going to consider it viable until a very good ultrasound told me both its gender and its singularity. We had resolved what to me was the most important issue at that point, the choice of a name. He could name a boy, and I could name a girl.

When I met him, all I knew was that his name was William Jones. "I'm Tragedy Jones," I'd said. "*My* mother needed to jack up the last name a little. Well, a *lot*."

"So, if you marry me, you won't fix any of your problems," he said.

"What?"

I hadn't dated anyone after that. But it had taken over six months before I learned he was William Shakespeare Jones V. He had been so embarrassed by his name that he had preferred to be forgettable. "Some great-great-great-grand-mother probably had heard of Shakespeare and thought that made her boy look intellectual," William said.

I didn't tell him why I liked the name. It already was pushing for him to know we had *one* name in common. I trusted he'd take classes in more contemporary dramaturgy and never think about the connection. Now that we were married it was a different story. Of course we would have a William Shakespeare Jones VI. Not only did that VI make him practically an aristocrat, but Shakespeare was a synonym for tragedy if I wanted him to be.

A girl baby would be another story. I quickly narrowed name choices to two. Esme and Mavis. I would tell everyone they were sentimental, and I would be the only one who knew better. I might not even tell William for a while. Esme was my friend who abhorred symmetry, but her name came from a story about a girl who was wise and lonely, but resilient. Mavis was Gammy's name. But Mavis was also Mavis Staples. William loved it when I told him. She was from Chicago, too.

"Ain't nobody cryin'," he sang in pure falsetto I didn't know he had. "I'll take you there."

I loved the word *staples*.

"Mavis Staples Jones," William said. "Another generation walking into a classroom with a teacher expecting a black child."

We already had some idea of what our child would look like. In general. William could have been the fraternal triplet, with the same nowhere-in-particular coloring we twins had. Honey-colored hair, chameleon green-gray eyes, facial features that individually couldn't be described to a sketch artist but together were excellent, I would have to admit. Mavis Staples Jones or William Shakespeare Jones VI would not surprise me or William but would surprise the kindergarten teacher who had seen the roll. Unless I was carrying twins.

***

I was carrying Mavis.

William and I had decided that when we told our families, we would disclose only that the baby was not a twin. We would let them be surprised about gender and name the day Mavis Staples Jones was born. We never explored why we were doing it that way. His parents were over a thousand miles away; it wasn't a matter of intrusion. I had ways of keeping intrusion away from us when my mother, grandmother, and sister lived within a mile of us. I figured it was my excitement over Gammy finding out. For all of my life, I knew that she was maybe one percent Gammy and ninety-nine percent Mavis. She had a world of being Mavis.

When we told them at the Chinese restaurant, Comedy was seated across the round table from me. Her eyes said, *We used to have secrets.*

All of them were at the hospital the day I went into labor. Each of them had come with me several times to my checkups. Dr. Jacobson had learned over years of experience how not to divulge secrets, and he had learned that sometimes there was no point in trying to clear out the delivery room. He was no more capable than I was of choosing two people to throw out.

Labor took long enough to be boring. No one would leave the room. "You'll know when it's about to happen," I said.

147

"It's not like a comet's coming, and you'll miss it if you blink." But no one would leave for food, no one would volunteer to fetch snacks. They were an odd group for small talk. My mother tried the subject of herself having twins. "They sliced you two out of me," she said. She focused on me. "It was your fault, Trage. You had your sister all twisted up."

"You are not being helpful," Gammy said.

"You could make this entertaining if you tell us the name," my mother said to William.

"I don't think we waited until now to make that news a time-killer," William said.

The nurse came to check me. I had no more idea of the progress of labor than my family did. Such was the greatness of the epidural.

"She's ready to push," the nurse said. "Are you sure you all want to be in here?"

"Nothing we haven't all seen before," my mother said.

"Hold on, Mama," Comedy said.

"Yours is just like it," my mother said.

"But not with a bloody baby coming out of it."

I beckoned Comedy to come stand by my head. Gammy chose to do the same. But my mother and husband were determined to be right there when the baby one of them knew as Mavis arrived. I thought she was expecting an imprinting duck.

With sleight of hand that came of experience, Dr. Jacobson whipped little Mavis out and maneuvered her so my mother didn't see her gender, but William could cut the cord, and then, all wrapped up, she was handed to me.

"Comedy, Mama, Gammy, I want you to meet Mavis Jones," I said.

"Oh my, oh my, oh my," Gammy said.

My mother peered at little Mavis intently, her eyes wide. "I can't believe it," she said in a reverent whisper. "She looks just like you when you were born. I mean *exactly*."

"Oh, thank God,"Comedy said.

FIG PRESERVES

Actually, it wasn't Annie, but rather Mrs. Shoot, who started the business of waiting every evening in the driveway. I liked it for a while. Peter was so small when I first had to leave him. And Mrs. Shoot had all the basics that add up to understanding new babies; that's why I chose her.

Waiting in the driveway was an elementary lesson for him, toddling and fumbling around, learning eventually that when the sun took a certain cast and Mrs. Shoot took him out, then I would come back. It all made perfect sense, Peter and I learning together about object permanency. At least when he was small enough to rein in. But the days got progressively shorter, and he got swifter, and the days lengthened and shortened again, and whatever solace came from my sure arrival slowly got less important for him. After a while I sensed that it was the time of day Mrs. Shoot looked forward to. For her own solace.

Now the ritual was decidedly different, and I knew my role had slipped into being the catalyst for breaking up a pleasant gathering. Now there were four of them, a tight but aimless unit. Every evening, six afternoons a week. Annie and James were the other two and, like Mrs. Shoot, they ceased to exist on Sundays. But when I got back from the coffee shop, a place of old niceties in slick new form, there they were. Mrs. Shoot was getting about as vague as Annie, and I had to be careful as I pulled in.

Peter and James had a way of zipping out of unlikely places, right into the path of the car. I tried never to think about it too much, because so far Peter never had had more than a scratch under Mrs. Shoot's care, and if I thought about it too much I was not going to be able to leave the house every day. All I could do was protect him from myself.

Annie was vague. She always had had vague eyes, gray-green eyes that were two lazy pools in her face, never drawing a person into anything. Since the accident, the vagueness was quite keen, though that's an odd thing to say. She could say memorable things, but they always came from places that were dark and disjointed and unconnected to what she ought to have been thinking about.

Part of the day's end ritual was for Annie to stand around, looking suddenly serious about watching James, and even

Peter, while I edged Mrs. Shoot away from the house. Mrs. Shoot and I had no perfect balance between us; I called her Mrs. Shoot and she called me Margaret. Though that wasn't as unbalanced as it could have been, for everyone else called me Marghi, and everyone else called her Mrs. Lillian Shoot. *MsLillianShoot.* I phoned her house, and her great-niece called her to the phone that way. Annie sensed the confoundedness of it all, I think, and always got away from us at evening's dismissal, especially on Saturdays, when I paid Mrs. Shoot and for a minute the power was in the right place.

It seemed to me that every day, after Mrs. Shoot left, Annie found her way into my house. Certainly that day she did. She was just standing in the driveway, watching James with a funny sort of control that made him never quite come to her, so all she could do was stay planted there. I invited her in, and the watch over James stopped immediately. Peter and James were at the back of my property, throwing each other to the ground and looking as if they were hurting each other, though neither complained. Annie made no move to corral them, so I took it upon myself. Peter started back right away, with that funny little-boy slow drag of feet that made him look as if he were slogging through mud. James was slower on the uptake, having no reason to answer my call. He stood up, dusted himself off only when it became clear to him that he wasn't going to have Peter to entertain him back there anymore.

"I bet you'd find bricks under here," Annie said, dragging the toe of her right foot in a small arc across one of the two dirt troughs that made up my driveway.

"How do you figure that?"

"I know these things."

Annie's knowledge came from strange places. I'd been told we might find brick walkways and pathways in our yard. Annie also might find them in hers. The houses mirror one another, built around 1880 to fill the needs of white people only a bit better off than the newly freed slaves who lived in the nearby shotguns.

Stephen and I always respected that our house had a history, and fragment by fragment we'd scraped down to what was original and bought period fixtures wherever they were missing. But Harry and Annie let the rot go, and after the accident Annie put in aluminum siding and windows and gutters, leaving solid color and straight lines in all the places where our house was sentimentally blurred by time.

I offered her coffee. It was partly reflex; offering coffee was what I did in my shop all day. It was also what a person was supposed to do. No matter that normal people were beginning to think about supper at that hour. No matter that Stephen was peevish the first few times he came home and found Annie sipping coffee in our kitchen, demure as she pleased. Eventually I'd begun fixing supper around her, and Stephen no longer had reason to be put out. Some days Annie would teeter out when I started piling up the plates, probably because what I was serving didn't appeal to her. Other days she would do nothing, sit there as vacant and ordinary as she could make herself. Those days, I said nothing, set a place for her, a place for James.

James came tearing into the kitchen just as I set the thick mug of coffee in front of his mother. His eyes had that red edge of anger that little boys get when they would give anything to be off in private and crying indignantly. "He hit me," I heard him whisper into Annie's neck, wet and sloppy and sad.

She stroked his head absently. Annie had that dark sort of hair that might have been blonde when she was small. Almost black with no red or gold in it. James was a towhead. Harry had the same color hair as Annie, only he had dark eyes while hers were light, so I figured she was the one he took after. I'd never bothered to ask.

Her fingers ran over the middle of his head, a few inches in front of the point on the crown where all his hair fell from. Right where the fontanel once was open. "Did you ever think about this spot when they were newborns?"

"I knew it was there, if that's what you mean." I was surprised. The origin of Annie's thoughts baffled me, but I saw one pattern, one consistency. It took me a while to pick up on it, but it had persisted for a couple of years, and I'd watched carefully. She never talked about anything that happened before the accident. This question was probably just a close call. Because Harry was killed when James was

154

nine months old, and I could no longer remember how old babies were before their skulls closed up. But I was sure James's head was not fine and solid by nine months; otherwise Annie would not have been talking about it.

***

It happened on a Sunday afternoon. It was the earliest part of the summer, before the heat was so oppressive that a person can be sick from it, before summer had hung on so long it was no longer good to have it. Peter and James were only weeks apart in age, and they were at that second good hurdle where a mother can grab some new equilibrium. My way of doing it was to sit in the shadow of the live oak that stood at the back of my house. I had a book to read, an Anne Tyler book finally after so many months of catching words only in snippets, scanning the newspaper on a quick break at the shop, flipping through lightweight magazines that could be held in one straining hand while holding a nursing baby with the other. It didn't matter that afternoon whether I read or not; I knew I could if I wanted to.

Annie's way of getting back to herself was to make some preserves. "Harry's going to get some figs," she called from her kitchen window with that sure, proprietary tone that comes of squatting in one place for a number of years. Our leaves blew across the property line in the fall, thick vines of poison oak crept into their yard sometimes in the late summer, so it was fair to lay claim to any fruit that grew

155

naturally on our lot. The tomatoes in Stephen's garden were another story. Annie always asked first before picking them.

We figured our fig tree went back as far as the history of our house. We didn't know anything about how fig trees grew, but it was sensible that a tree of such dimensions would go back more than a hundred years. Our fig tree looked like those pictures I'd seen of the African baobabs, gnarled and ancient and crazy-dead-looking when winter came. A person would have to climb quite a distance up into it before he had to test the branches.

My eyes were closed, and my hearing was that much keener. I was listening for Peter to stir in the playpen on the grass. The playpen was pumpkin-yellow plastic, handed down in several families of otherwise fine taste. He was still, squirming just often enough to let me know he was all right. I could hear the chunking of garden shears by Mr. Haas, whose lot backed up to ours. His lot was deep, too, so the distance from his front property line to our front property line was the full span of the block. He never surfaced much, just clipped the hedge at the back when it looked too messy. That happened about three times a summer, fewer times the rest of the year.

After Annie called out, I heard Harry come out their back door, scuffle across their patchy back yard and across our thick St. Augustine, and disappear with a rustle or two into the fig tree. It was getting hot, even in the shade, and I was thinking that maybe it was not good for Peter to be out in that much heat. I thought of moving him closer to the house; I thought of moving myself, too. Then, in the quiet punctuated only by the sound of Mr. Haas's shears, I heard the slightest motion in the fig tree, maybe a few branches, followed by the sound of something large, solid, and quiescent hitting the ground near the tree. I almost didn't bother to look.

He was dead on the ground. Mr. Haas came vaulting over the hedge, defying age and gravity. Stephen came running from the front yard after I began to scream, and Annie was out last, a red and white dish towel still in her hand. Mr. Haas and Stephen didn't know much about heroic measures, but if they had suspicions that Harry was dead they ignored them. Annie just stood there; the one clear thing I remember about that afternoon was that Annie just stood there.

While Stephen and Mr. Haas shook Harry and loosened his clothes and begged him to come around, while the paramedics bagged him and paddled him, while the police came and did their orderly things, even when the ambulance came and took him away, James was screaming in the house, but Annie just stood there, and I finally came back to enough good sense to creep into her house and bring James out, placing him in the playpen with Peter.

Otherwise, I never left the yard myself, and I don't know how Stephen and Mr. Haas managed for everything to be taken care of, but right before the ambulance arrived Harry's partner from the law firm pulled up into our driveway and took Annie over. I saw her at the funeral, but I was protected by the crowd and the formality, and I didn't have to deal with the fact that her husband had fallen dead on the ground from the tree in my yard.

The night of the funeral, Stephen lay next to me in the bed in the light. I was staring at the ceiling, knowing absolutely I was not going to go to sleep, trying to think of what was right and what was going to be easiest.

"You heard nothing, right?" he said, and I nodded without looking to see whether he saw. "So he was probably dead before he fell."

"We'll see," I said.

I waited for days, watching Annie's house before I came or went. But she never came out much, at least never at the times when I needed to come and go. Though my life always had been orderly where hers had not, and it seemed after a few days that if she was watching me, too, then it was certainly easier for her to make sure we never passed each other outside. I knew I was going to gather the decency to go over and speak to her, but I wanted to wait and see what she would do to me about our tree.

Keeping watch, I had noticed she had visitors. Harry's partner came a lot, at proper times of the day and never for more than an hour. Other familiar sorts came, too, people I remembered from the only party Annie and Harry ever gave, a Christmas gathering for Harry's office staff. Stephen and I had been invited, I figured, because social amenities were new to Annie, and she saw this party as a big, noisy nuisance that we'd complain about if we weren't there.

No noise seeped out into the neighborhood, and we didn't need to be there, but I talked to a few of the same people who now were dropping in on Annie. I didn't recall what they had talked about at a party five months past, though I assumed it was real estate and politics, but I did recognize their faces. I'd been grateful for their attention, having challenged myself to tough it out for an hour even though Stephen had begged me to leave. Now they were closing in the ranks, I imagined, planning with Annie to take Stephen and me and our insurers for all we were worth.

Three weeks passed, with no letter, no official phone call, no subpoena, and I thought about going to see Annie. I might offer to keep James, try to normalize. But she came over first. "We'll need to use your driveway," she said, standing at my side door.

"Sure," I said. Anything.

"It'll only be a few days, I hope," she said, and she left. That was when they put the siding on her house. And the windows. And the gutters. It took two weeks, but I didn't complain. Annie got a new car and she began hanging out with Mrs. Shoot in the driveway, and she'd been coming in for coffee and thoughts out of the blue for so long that it was natural as could be.

***

She continued to stroke James's head. "No, I mean, were you ever tempted by the terrible vulnerability of it?"

James slid off her lap, headed back into the part of the house where he had left Peter, and after a while I heard the back door slam shut. It was dusk, but the floodlights in the yard were on the timer, so we never had too little light out there. I sat looking at Annie, wondering even after all this time what I might say, but knowing it was a matter of minutes before something came out of her, something that wouldn't make me think until hours later.

The back door slammed again, and I heard footsteps come through the house; they were close enough to stomps that I knew the mission was important.

"James's in the fig tree," Peter screeched. "James's in the fig tree!"

I rose from my chair so fast I knocked the table, sending a gulp-worth of coffee sloshing out of my mug. But Annie didn't move. She reached for my arm, casually, just enough to get my attention. "Don't worry," she said. "Really, don't worry."

UNDER THE BELLJAR

People always remember my screen name. Belljar01. It was good after the storm when everyone was scattered without electronic memories, and the only way to be found was by frantic web postings — or by e-mail sent up to the memorable ones. That's probably how that Mariah kept track of me. I met her in January, and I made a point of telling her my screen name so she'd know I wasn't a simple aborigine. I worried she was down here looking at us as some kind of hapless civilization who couldn't explain ourselves. The night I met her she asked me if I knew the Transylvanian. Andrei Perlmutter wasn't a native, running around in costume with little provocation, but he sure wasn't a Transylvanian.

I'm Belljar because I had Sylvia Plath's room when I was

a junior at Smith. The third-floor single in Haven House, guaranteed to make anyone slightly mad. I'm glad to explain that to anyone who asks, and they always ask because they want me to know they suspect me of being suicidal. It's my way of telling them that, yes, I'm pretty chronically depressed, but also that I got away from New Orleans once or twice. My official biography, well, unofficial but the one I give out, says I've lived my whole life in New Orleans except for slight interruptions for education and natural disasters. I was pretty much dragged kicking and screaming out of town for both. Nobody knows I went to college kicking and screaming because I smiled at the airport and got Massachusetts and its smells deep into my memory. But I've told everybody that I did not want to be hauled off to Texas after Katrina. I stayed in my house for two weeks and only left because my brother had gone to the trouble to send in a friend with a truck to remind me that I had no food and no way to get any. Wading through four feet of water wasn't worth the large number of supermarkets in Texas. I came back as soon as a grocery opened in Jefferson Parish. Electricity or not. I'm sixth-generation here. And maybe thoroughly traumatized because we all are. But that would have been no reason for Mariah to have been down here studying me and the rest of us at arm's length and having someone pay for her to do so.

Mariah was at the reopening of the bookshop on Pirates Alley, and she looked so sincere. No one else seemed sincere, least of all me. I was there because I was asked to read. I wasn't celebrating. I frankly didn't care about anything happening in the French Quarter. The French Quarter wasn't New Orleans. I read a poem, and no one paid attention. It was about Mr. Williams the snowball man on Plum Street. Kids in the '60s figured he smuggled drugs.

The poem wasn't what they wanted. A writer named Roy got up and talked about walking around the Quarter with a poodle, and everyone was rich and happy and full of whoops. Mariah seemed baffled, so I assumed she understood everything. I caught her eye, something I hadn't known to do when I was reading, and I caught her eye again when a writer whose name I didn't know read a preposterous little scene of New Orleans under water like ancient Alexandria. No one listened. Rich people don't have time for phonies; I'll give them credit for that.

I thought Mariah was catching my eye because she enjoyed the silence even more than she scoffed at the story. I walked out with her, told her yes, everybody knows the man with the Romanian accent, learned within the half block to her parked bike that she was here from North Carolina, invited her to my house. No, she said, but she would meet me for coffee. In the Quarter. I offered to give her a ride if she wanted to visit me one day.

She wasn't venturing past the lights, she told me. But there are no lights in the daytime, I said. We both know where they are, she said. I laughed. I knew what she meant. I challenged myself sometimes back then. Hollygrove, for instance, looked inhabited during the day. The double shotgun houses were intact.

There were a normal number of cars parked on the streets. But if I drove through at night, the only lights were my headlights. No other vehicle passed, no house had a single bulb burning. No barrooms were open. For all I knew, electricity had been restored. But the people weren't there. And the cars didn't run. I pretended I was a child, though capable of driving, of course, and I scared myself silly. But I couldn't speed. I'd tear the holy hell out of my wheels. I took my fun where I found it. I still didn't have cable television back.

Mariah met me at the CC's in the lower end of the Quarter. I do love the Quarter, I just don't consider it New Orleans. Nobody black lives in the Quarter, except a few gays, a few bourgie types, and worst of all, a few bourgie gay types. Though at the time almost nobody black lived anywhere in the city. Nobody who was born here lives in the Quarter (except maybe Lindy Boggs and the woman who owns Arnaud's.)

The Quarter's on high ground: that's why it's so *old*. And that's why it's so *intact*. I didn't want to patronize the Quarter. I didn't want Mariah coming to New Orleans and telling anybody that she'd seen New Orleans because she'd seen only the Quarter.

"Tell me about yourself," I said, which of course was my way of saying that at some point I wanted to hold forth on my own story. I already knew a little about her from having ordered. Mariah was skinny under her fine-knit sweater, with terrific pipestem arms, and she didn't think twice about ordering a large mocha with whole milk, not a word of Italian jargon, and a slab of carrot cake. She plunked down a ten for her food, not even considering the possibility of niceties. I pegged her right away as having no ability to sit still. I liked that.

"I'm here on assignment," she said.

Not that it mattered, but I didn't believe her. She didn't seem that spectacular. New Orleans was oozing words. To be paid to be here, she would have to have been spectacular. She read me. "Well, it's on spec," she said. "But I'm not finding anything ordinary. I'm practically guaranteed a story."

I looked around. We were in a coffee shop drinking what we wanted and at four other tables people were working on laptops. At the CC's uptown, people were sitting on the pavement working on laptops. That was it. The shop uptown was closed, but the wi-fi inside was thrumming away. Maybe somebody outside might be drinking a Diet Coke, but that was it. On the pavement. "This is ordinary," I said, waving my hand around.

She had seen a second line, she told me, stepped into the moving crowd, caught a rhythm she didn't know she had. She had taken her car down to the Lower Nine, seen that barge that breached the levee, in person, herself, just like on television, tracked the rush of the water in her mind. I gave her a questioning look.

It was past the lights, she admitted, but she had done it the second day in town, and it was her reason for not venturing beyond the sliver by the river any anymore. She felt too hyperbolic out there.

"I like you," I said. I thought maybe she was going to take her time writing about New Orleans. Taking her time gave her the possibility of digging down to the spirit of the place. She would have to find a way not to mention food and music and water if she wanted to get it right, and for that she was going to have to take time. Since she looked like she had a sense of humor, I was willing to give her a chance. Really, all New Orleans has that no other city has is a sense of humor. I asked her if she had seen those funny T-shirts.

"Make levees, not war?" she said.

"Those are all right," I said. By all right I meant acceptable. Not funny the way I needed funny. "I was thinking of the ones that say, 'I survived Katrina, and all I got was this lousy T-shirt and a plasma TV and a Cadillac Escalade.'"

She hesitated. "Looters?" I nodded. She smiled.

"Though the Cadillac Escalade part was the police."

She pulled out a notebook.

"It's an old story. Don't even bother with it. A policeman evacuated in a Cadillac he liberated from the dealership. It's old enough to be a joke. That's the way this whole thing has to be. Old enough to be a frigging joke."

She said she would come to my house when she came past the lights. It took her a few months. Her e-mail was breathless. "I saw a fire!" She had seen a helicopter with an 800-gallon bucket drop water on a downtown fire and had pedaled madly on her bicycle toward it, and before she knew it she was out in all the neighborhoods all the time. Fire was all it had taken. She could have learned all she needed to know about the city by touring the burned-out hulls and stopping to talk, getting invited in, it seemed to me.

I'd watched the horizon as the two mansions on Carrollton went up and burned to the ground the week after the storm when even the fire station was under four feet of water. Behind them lay Hollygrove. No need for disaster tours, just fire tours, a special way to see the city. The helplessness behind the helplessness. The firemen couldn't do their job. We were leaking millions of gallons of water every day in broken pipes underground. We were oozing rich metaphors. She could have a story full of irony. Fire, not water. But all Mariah needed was that one fire. For her it was excitement. She was ready to roam the streets.

"Your house is adorable," Mariah said, looking into my living room, and I said, "Okay." I had half a house, sliced horizontally. A raised cottage, its unfinished basement had been gutted long-distance from Houston where I sat glassy-eyed, money mailed to honest Hondurans, all my memories set on the curb. The upstairs was the same as it had been before the storm, but it was freezing. I had water in the gasline. I needed a very strong male to open the pipe and empty the drip leg, I told her. I thought that was funny, even though I'd been in four layers of clothing for two days, waiting for a shift in the weather or my nephew or Entergy or, rarest or rarities, a plumber. "Write it down," I said. "Drip leg! I get maybe half a cupful of water in this section of pipe, and my heat shuts off. But it sounds like something connected to a prostate, don't you think? Nobody outside of here knows about drip legs!"

She was standing at the threshold of my house. She didn't want to come in. She had a car. I guessed I couldn't blame her for not wanting to sit and be cold, but there was nowhere to have coffee anywhere near where I live. Nothing had reopened. I suggested PJ's out in Metairie. They were open four hours a day. I had learned these things. PJ's was near my psychiatrist's office.

My psychiatrist was losing her mind. She was one of only 22 in the whole city, and she could have seen four people an hour, 24 hours a day, and still have turned patients away. The entire metropolitan region was insane. That was a good story. I could show her office to Mariah. Mariah could see Northline. "I don't know about Metairie," she said. I told her she should. But she was here to write about New Orleans.

"Can we walk around and talk to people on the streets?" she said. She liked being out in Treme, where she might get called white bitch, or she might sit on a stoop and drink beer and feel like a native.

In the past, the only people I'd ever seen out on the streets in Old Metairie were joggers, and the security patrol probably knew them by name and address. Since Northline got its extremely democratic hosing from the flood, I hadn't seen one person outdoors except construction crews. Those houses had a maximum of a quarter-million in insurance, but their owners easily went into their pockets for the two million in repairs. I wanted Mariah to see how fair Katrina was.

We sat in PJ's, and she said, "I'll definitely write about this."

"Helicopters took people off of roofs on Northline," I said. I knew a couple personally. I knew they went to the airport and lay for three days on the floor before flying to Dallas. I didn't mention that they found a quite fine three-bedroom apartment. That didn't matter. The husband was still in the hospital. In Dallas. He wasn't getting over the heat. I figured he was going to die. Probably before he got back to New Orleans. And not to his house.

I'd shown Mariah his house. It was surrounded by dead foliage. Everything was dead on Northline. Money didn't buy Northline into Oz. I'd tried out the Kansas line on her. She hadn't written it down, but I figured it was so good she'd remember it.

I saw Mariah surprisingly often in the months after that. I say surprisingly because my way of being a regular New

Orleans person who saw a psychiatrist was to stay at home. But my friend Sarah's way was to run around taking photographs. Sarah had lost everything in the storm, house, car, cat, everything. She had gotten on a plane to Atlanta two days before, the way one kind of sane person would have, had left a week's worth of food for her cat the way one kind of sane person would have. She put all her art, all her studio supplies, on high shelves. Covered it all with plastic.

Again, she was a sane person. Maybe we would get six inches of water. Maybe her roof wouldn't hold. She'd be back on Wednesday. Now Sarah was constructively sane, living in a studio apartment with a digital camera and four changes of clothes, a laptop from which she sent me every photo so they'd all float in cyberspace, no commitments. Certainly she had no land line.

"I can carry my entire life onto a plane; I don't even need to check it," she would say to anyone she met, and she met a lot of people when she took photographs. I thought she was an enviable kind of sane. So I went out with her to try to catch the contagion of motion. We were close to Sarah's gutted house on a Tuesday afternoon in April when we saw Mariah shouting to a man working a backhoe with all his might, trying to move one tree trunk from the middle of a block to the end of that block. He seemed terribly interested in failing.

I invited Mariah in to see Sarah's house. "It's not gutted to the studs," I said. Sarah had saved as many of her own artistic touches as she could. The ceramic backsplash was still in its place where the kitchen had been. Stained glass windows hadn't blown out in the bathroom. The fireplace stood free with most of her hand-painted tiles holding their pattern. It was possibly the most personal house I knew in the city before the storm. I'd sometimes asked Sarah what would happen when she left the house, and it was unspoken and wicked that I was asking about her being carried out as an old, dead woman.

"I don't go inside," Mariah said.

"Hey, I don't pay liability insurance for my health," Sarah said.

I looked at Mariah to see whether she would write that down. She didn't have her notebook out, so I figured she'd remember it. "She has to keep up her homeowner's, too," I said. "And her flood. Can you imagine?" Mariah looked bored. "What," I said.

"Oh, you know," she said. "I want to make this about New Orleans. You know, the interesting part."

I didn't say anything.

Mariah looked apologetic. Sarah was level-headed. She just waited.

"Look, I'm sorry," Mariah said. "I have to have vivid images, that's all. If I talk about insurance policies, I'll put people to sleep."

"So come on inside the house," I said.

"I never go inside," Mariah said. "I told myself when I started that it's really all on the street."

I told her Sarah now can fit everything she owns into an overhead compartment on a plane. "Think about it," I said. "We really could fit the entire city into the Convention Center now — with everything we have."

Sarah started to laugh. It was a terrific laugh, such a good laugh, in fact, that Mariah laughed, too.

After that day I got several e-mails from Mariah, and though they could have come from anywhere, they came from New Orleans. She stayed and stayed and never published her story. I pictured her standing in front of a conveyor belt, old story facts falling off one edge as new ones came along. All those early months here were wasted, but it seemed to me that she would be hard-pressed to find anything to say about New Orleans now.

New Orleans was *all* about insurance now. Everybody was indoors. But I was happy because New Orleans was funny as hell in the saddest way. The mayor was under his bed and the congressman who was re-elected handily was being indicted for what his real self would have called pure-D greed. We were fools. Hilarious, even if only to ourselves. But none of it was in the
streets, none of it had to do with food or music or water. Still, Mariah found a lot of fried seafood and warm beer, obscure local bands who told her they were famous. She helped some

Episcopalians gut a house, she told me, and she imagined what it was like to drown in that house.

"I went inside," she said. "And now I'm just completely ruined. But those were people I couldn't tell no."

The last e-mail I got from her was in late summer. A tropical storm named Ernesto looked as if it was heading this way. It never crossed my mind to leave town. I had told my brother that I would evacuate if anything like a slow category 2 or a fast 3 came this way, and Ernesto showed no signs that I even needed batteries for my flashlight. But Mariah wrote me from North Carolina.

"I guess I've been around voodoo too long," she wrote. "I took it as a sign that my time there was over."

"I see the irony hasn't worn off of you," I wrote her back. I didn't say that I hadn't seen any on her up to that moment. "Sustain it as you write. For everyone in New Orleans, it's all I ask."

I didn't expect her to write. I'd seen over time enough of her clothes. If she was writing on spec, the person who was speculating that she was going to write something was a loving daddy.

It was a year after I met Mariah, and months after I'd forgotten about her, that Sarah called me to say she'd sold the photo. *Hodge's* Magazine was giving her the cover for the July issue and paying her more than she'd ever made for any piece of art. She was mystified by their choice, an old photo by post-Katrina standards, one dating to about two months after the storm. "I'm past that; isn't everyone past that?" she said. It showed the mountain of debris on the neutral ground at West End. At the time it had seemed as if all the people who once lived in Lakeview had all their possessions in that mound. It wasn't an aesthetic photograph. Not even in an abstract expressionist kind of way. Sarah had taken it as a snapshot, she had been the first to admit. "Someone's rehashing some very old stuff," she said. We went to dinner on the strength of her check.

The someone was Mariah. I found out when Sarah got her advance copy, and she only showed it to me because she figured I'd see it eventually. She was wrong in that I don't read *Hodge's,* but right because eventually three people had no problem calling and telling me they knew I was BJ.

We are not even as evolved as aborigines. We are animals in the wild that Mariah has studied, and she has given us names to show she has been able to distinguish us from one another. Gorilla from gorilla, elephant from elephant. BJ, the Romanian, Reefer, Prep. Having sorted us out so cleverly, she was sure she also had figured out everything she needed to know about us in the first four months she was here. As I read, I saw that her chronology didn't even give us the grace to have recovered a full year. She could use so much more drama by extrapolating from the big three — food, music, water — and telling all her stories about fire, gunshots, alcohol, and strange rituals. Never once did she have to step into anyone's home. A bar, yes. A church, all right. But never a home, even if it was possible to see daylight through it all the way, front to back.

"I've seen fire, I've seen rain, I've seen sunny days that I thought would never end," she quoted, to get the reader singing.

Her preference was to think she was stepping inside people. And she stepped inside me.

"New Orleans is rebuilding its bricks and mortar. But some of its people who have withstood the test of time did not wash away, and they're still standing in the ruins. Take BJ for instance. She is under psychiatric care. There are only twenty-two psychiatrists in the region practicing, so she must be an extreme case, but possibly emblematic of why New Orleans may never recover. I am no diagnostician, but I would guess she is manic-depressive. Her e-mail screen name is synonymous with "suicide." Yet for her everything about Katrina is a joke. She won't talk about the storm unless it's a joke. She can't take it seriously. She has to laugh.

"BJ's everything that is wrong with New Orleans. 'Manic-depression is my diagnosis for the city. How can they have Mardi Gras and Jazzfest when half the population is in exile?

"BJ will tell you upon first meeting that she is sixth-generation New Orleanian. With people who cling so desperately to the past, New Orleans will never face the future."

I don't think I want to see my psychiatrist anymore.

175

First publication was in *Life in the Wake* (NOLAFugees Press, 2007) Reprinted with permission.

REAL ESTATE

The evening had all the making of a fine memory. Andrew had made reservations at the steak house on North Broad. That's where I took him the first time he came to New Orleans and I was trying to seduce him. Not into my bed, because I wouldn't use food that way, but into wanting New Orleans. It was before the steak house became a chain. A porterhouse and fresh asparagus, which had nothing to do with life in New Orleans: that was all it took to astonish him.

He decided to move here and marry me, and he'd eaten well over the years, no complaints. Of course New Orleans gave him many other reasons to complain, and then he would remind me that if it were not for me he could be living in North Carolina or New Mexico or just about any place where it was possible to go out after dark and come home alive. Or to do business on merit. Or to drive a car like a sane person. I tended to agree, though I never said so. I couldn't.

I thought we were celebrating. We'd gone to act of sale on the house in the morning, and even though life was now sloppy, it was a pivotal point. We were living in my high-school friend's guest room near Tulane, around the corner from our sold house, with all our furniture in storage because the house was bought faster than we found a new one. We had remarkably few boxes to store because Andrew had gone on a tear. "Selling before buying almost *never* happens," our agent had said, practically asking us to congratulate her. I sensed it wasn't all that much about her speed, but I didn't know why. Andrew had told the agent to price it to sell, and I had said, "Well, of course." It wasn't that we were smart. It was something else.

I ordered a Grey Goose and tonic, and I planned to have as many as I wanted. If Andrew had too many, we'd take a taxi. I wanted pure pleasure tonight. I wanted mushrooms broiled in butter. The house had meant responsible life. Bedrooms for children. A dining room table big enough for six every night. A full attic. A full attic had been a commitment. We had been the old people. Now we were moving back toward romance. Andrew had told me that having no rooms for the children to come back to was a good thing. Our youngest was finished college now. I thought Andrew was going to make a quiet toast before the food came.

Instead he handed me a check. He didn't bother to put it in an envelope, just pulled it from the inside pocket of his suit coat and handed it to me, face up. It was made out to me from an account I didn't know he had, and the amount was ninety-thousand dollars. I squealed with delight because I thought this was discretionary money for me to play with, that it was a good surprise. "Hold on," he said, and he pulled the check back. "I don't think you get it."

He actually made me play a game. "Think; what's the significance of ninety-thousand dollars? Doesn't twice that amount ring a bell?" He sounded almost angry that I hadn't gotten his message, almost as if he wouldn't have done it if I'd understood to begin with. Yes, all right, it was easy to recall that we had a hundred-eighty thousand dollars in equity from the house after the mortgage was paid off. So this was my half.

***

That was his way of saying goodbye. After I had ordered sixty dollars' worth of food I couldn't eat. *Here is not enough money for you to do anything, but clearly I've been to a bank, so I've been to a lawyer, too; goodbye.* He didn't need to explain himself. He didn't need to give reasons, but I asked why, and for that I was just as wrong as I'd been when I'd misunderstood the reason for the check. So he answered why by blaming me.

I was boring. That was the sum of it. I had two more

vodkas and felt less and less boring, but he said nothing different. "You don't do anything," he said. "But I *am* something," I said, looking into his CPA eyes.

That was in May. I kicked him out of my friend's apartment, so it only took me one day to find out that I wasn't boring after all. He took his clothes and went straight to Sarah's house. Sarah had what I figured was a boring house because it was in Lakeview, and right away without thinking Andrew gave her all of his ninety-thousand dollars, and Andrew legally owned half interest in a house in Lakeview. He had a writ of some kind that made sure I didn't own half of his half while he was getting rid of me. I figured Sarah must have been very exciting for him to seize her that way while he was still not clear of me.

I think of Andrew every day now because I hate him every day because my knees hurt every day. It's been three months, and of course I'm living the way I would be if it were three months past the May when I married Andrew — which was almost thirty years ago. I have about as much going for me as any unskilled twenty-three-year-old. Except that I'm not lithe enough to work this way. I work at Barnes & Noble in Metairie, and I'm expected to squat and lift and carry like anyone else who deserves eight dollars an hour.

William doesn't know about my knees. He's thirty-eight, and I know he likes to move as close to me as possible. He's worked at Barnes & Noble for five years, and he knows the bureaucracy, so he can get himself assigned to my hours and my work area. I would have a crush right back on him if I dared think of myself as not boring. We are having our lunch break together today. Everyone is nervous. Not just in the store. Everywhere I go.

A piddling sort of hurricane has come across the Florida panhandle and is now in the Gulf of Mexico with nowhere to go but landfall. I personally think everyone in the store has a subliminal wish for a giant wind storm to destroy the store and leave us all on unemployment. I have an explicit wish for this to happen. Even though I have found myself, to my private shame, living not particularly far from the store, in Metairie, and the wind would destroy my house, too. I grew up in New Orleans. So did my mother and grandmother.

No one in my family ever has lived in Jefferson Parish. Actually no one in my family ever has lived outside of 70118, which was New Orleans, 18, Louisiana, when I was born. My mother and grandmother could not have located a street in Jefferson Parish to save themselves. Now I live in *new* Metairie, the ticky-tacky part of Jefferson Parish, because that is all I can afford. I put my check into a tiny salt box of a house near the lake, with wood siding painted pink, and I am surviving and hating Andrew on the other side of the parish line, finishing out his life in a full-commitment two-person house with this Sarah, who is not boring. I have checked Sarah on the Internet, and she has two citations on Google, a fact I'm sure Andrew would throw at me if he gets a chance. She shows up on lists at accounting conferences. Twice. Both times in the Midwest. She and Andrew must talk a lot about tax law. Barnes & Noble has three shelves of do-it-yourself tax books. Next year I will do my taxes myself, probably without a book. William thinks this is wonderful. William has a master's degree in fine arts, and he files the short form.

"Come with me to Baton Rouge," he says as the hurricane approaches. "Better yet, caravan with me. Unless you leave your car somewhere." He looks at me straight and hard. "I'd like you to leave your car somewhere. The airport, maybe." He sounds terribly romantic. In disasters, airports always are romantic.

I never evacuate for hurricanes. I was in middle school for Hurricane Betsy, and while the city was damaged downtown, and wind knocked out power all over the place, my mother's house was unscathed. She lost small tree limbs, but I was big enough to help pick them up. Her neighbor, whose house was on the corner, lost power, so my mother ran an extension cord out the kitchen window, and the neighbor kept her refrigerator running. That was it. My memories are total and accurate. Last year for Ivan, Andrew insisted we should leave. I let him get into the traffic to Houston by himself. I don't think I was boring to have done that.

I tell William that I have grown children all over the place, but then I amend that to say they're children past the age of majority because *grown* sounds too close to where he is. My children think I am a character. I am something because I did nothing: they all have told their friends that I let their father sweat and curse all the way across southern Louisiana while I sat in front of the television with a diet Coke and flipped between The Learning Channel and The Weather Channel, gleaning from the Learning Channel that Noah in the Old Testament probably only had a few dozen species on board and from the Weather Channel that the storm came in at Gulf Shores, Alabama. My children are in parts of California and Washington, DC, too far away to offer refuge. They also are too young to offer refuge. But they are just the right age to enjoy my refusal to leave town. They're not afraid for me because they trust me. I'm not sure why they're not afraid for their father.

"I never leave," I say. "And I've always been right."

"Haven't you always lived close to the river?" William says. He clearly has paid a lot of attention to my stories. It doesn't make me nervous at all.

He has a point. When I was in school, no one did anything about hurricanes except the kids who lived in the brand-new houses at the lakefront. Their parents checked into the Roosevelt Hotel.

I decide to go with William to Baton Rouge for the same reason I did not go to Houston with Andrew. It is sexy. I won't ask any questions, and that will be sexy as hell.

***

He has friends from graduate school who didn't wean themselves from the school, so life for them is mostly about alcohol and marijuana. They can teach three composition classes and write short stories and have circles under their eyes and live in apartment complexes and beg William to come back. If he has a friend who has deviated from the norm and married and found a job with benefits, he doesn't mention it.

We are driving in relatively speedy traffic, and we are going to stay with someone named Chesley who lives on College Drive and who said to bring sleeping bags. I haven't owned a sleeping bag since my children had them. Four of them, each with its own distinctive smell. The sleeping bags were among the many mementos Andrew insisted on throwing away when we packed up the house. William says he will share his sleeping bag, and while I know what that means, I say that a long time ago I figured out that a good comforter does the same trick. I try not to be too smart of a mother as I pack. I'm sure this Chesley thinks he can get all of his protein from beer. I pack vodka.

Within an hour of arrival, I have counted heads and sleeping places, and I know that William chose Chesley's apartment for sexual tension. I am not the only woman, and I am not the only one who looks as if she is not looking forward to the ambiguity of late darkness. Talk is not difficult, because the television is centered for Chesley's solitary life, so it is also centered for his crowd, and we honor silence for CNN a lot of the time, most of us having come from New Orleans and wondering if we can go home tomorrow. I feel as if I can stay awake all night if the television says I can go home tomorrow. But this is not your standard drama that will resolve itself at fifty-eight minutes after the hour. It goes on and on, and I don't involve myself in cooking because I would be too fastidious. I also don't involve myself in eating, for the same reason.

A lot of cooking has been done in Chesley's kitchen over a number of years, it seems, none of it by Chesley. The vodka, sent down more easily with a clean bottle of 7-Up, works fast, and I am not going to be able to stay up all night. "Where can I sleep?" I say to William around midnight, when I no longer care much about this Category 5 hurricane that is going to miss New Orleans and probably send us home tomorrow afternoon. He says he, too, is sleepy. He doesn't sound sleepy, but he does sound soft, and that's close enough. I'm not dexterous enough to make a good rectangle folded in half of my comforter, but William does it, and he places his sleeping bag alongside it. He has chosen a place for us, in Chesley's office, where so far no one is camping or sitting or even using the computer. I think there are about nine people staying here. I lie down in my clothes, ready to fall asleep, but I am grateful enough not to lie with my back to William's sleeping bag, so when he lies down, too, he leans right over and kisses me.

"Oh, no," I whisper, right into the kiss, which I hold onto and keep on tasting and loving and giving back. "Mmm," I finally say, and I pull away. "Not here," I say.

"Why?" he says.

"It's Baton Rouge," is all I can think to say, but he smiles because it makes a lot of sense to him. We go to sleep full of alcohol, and in the night Chesley doesn't lose electricity.

Oddly, he doesn't lose it until after the storm has passed into northern Mississippi and we have begun to hear rumors that the levees have been breached in New Orleans. I am packed and ready to go back to my house, and William and I are still drunken virgins. I am thinking after all this danger that my house might be a good place to go beyond kissing. Might. But what if I walk in and say, "It's Jefferson Parish"? I never have made love in Jefferson Parish. I suppose I will know what I can do.

William reasons that New Orleans is flooding, and Metairie is not, and since we are hot and miserable and lacking creature comforts in Baton Rouge, we might as well go back to my house. He knows for an absolute fact that his head is clear, and that it will be even clearer if he can get into an air-conditioned car and drive down an interstate. The trip is neither slow nor fast.

We are the only vehicle on the road for many stretches, but the highway is strewn with debris, and I think some agency of the government is not doing its job until I remember that, oh yes, we probably have no government. William can't drive the normal route to my house because trees block streets and strange objects lie in our path, a Mary-on-the-half-shell, a once-white wicker bassinet. It doesn't take us long to realize that we can ignore one-way signs. Really, we can ignore stop signs. But William stops at corners; he says it's important to him.

My house has running water and the gas works if I turn on the stove. It is unscathed. But there's no electricity, and the phone is dead. This is as good as Chesley's, if we discount the fact that we have not seen one person since we came off the interstate. "We don't need other people," William says. "I like supermarket checkers a lot," I say. William considers this piece of information, pulls his chest out, says in a deep voice, "I am a hunter-gatherer." I give him a go-on look. "We know there's food in Baton Rouge, and probably closer. I can range across *that* savannah."

"I like gas station attendants, too," I say.

We compromise and think we will stay for a week, rationing everything, canned food, gasoline, passion. Our understanding is that we do not make love because so far we have known each other as soap-fresh, always in air-conditioning. This is what I tell William. I can wash up at dawn and feel musky by eight. I say that is not how I want to be with William. I think he doesn't mind how he might be with me, but he doesn't want me to be that way with him. For my sake, not his. We can kiss all we want. Mouths can always be sweet.

We pilfer and loot and siphon and leave IOUs the second week. We can't go too far because now the 82nd Airborne is here, or others in uniform are here, and where men who want to exert authority are absent, nature still is in our way. Literally at the city line, there's still a flood. William lives near where I used to live, and he's pretty sure the flood doesn't go all the way to the river because nothing goes all the way to the river, but he can't get in to see. We go to the airport and retrieve my car, which is full of gasoline, and we're not sure our possibilities have grown with more gasoline.

Last night William told me that if something doesn't change in three days—an arbitrary choice—he will go back to Baton Rouge and board a plane to some city that he will choose within the next three days. He was not threatening; he was hoping I would come to my senses and join him. This morning at three-twenty-three the electricity came on.

That was all it took.

We have normalcy inside this house. We are clean, and we can stay clean. That means I can move past William unselfconsciously for many hours into the day. We can leave the house, too. If anyone were living nearby, we could know; we could hear air conditioning humming. We could sense nearby normalcy. But what heartens William is that there is possible electricity for many miles around.

"We might see an air-conditioned store soon," he says. "People in houses, working and shopping in stores. That's all we need."

I'm sure that trucks loaded with bananas—I don't know why I think it's bananas—are waiting at the Texas line. I tell him I want the gas pumps to operate. I like to be learning things. I think it's strange to have discovered that gasoline pumps operate on electricity. I'm sure he thinks we'll make love soon.

The water has receded in parts of New Orleans, and the mayor has made a glassy-eyed invitation for people to come home. There's another hurricane in the Gulf of Mexico, and I know he's crazy, but I think William and I should spend our first normal afternoon driving around and looking so we will have intense things to talk about in bed tonight. I think that will make a difference. He wants to see his apartment. I want to see Andrew's house. Andrew's house is closer. We go there first.

The streets of Lakeview are completely empty of people. With a car, we cannot get within ten blocks of where I know his house is. So we leave the car and walk, not worried about thieves. This is not wind debris in the streets. Water has pushed the guts out of houses, and it hasn't differentiated between street and curb. A grand piano is on a lawn. A car is on a fence. Entire living rooms are in the middles of streets.

"This is terrible," I say, and I mean it, even though I find myself fighting the tiny morbid smile that children get when they see blood.

"Have you seen enough?" William says. "You probably can extrapolate."

I tell him no. I've never seen Andrew's house, and this, perversely, is my chance.

We find the address, which I've learned by heart from forwarding and wrangling. It's two stories and a half, so the main part of the house sits on the ground, a few more rooms are up a half-story, and a little room is on a higher level. I'm surprised that it has this much character. The water line is eight feet high; I can see the brown mark across the front of the house. The National Guard and the ASPCA have been through this entire area and painted hieroglyphics on all the doors after kicking them in and looking for survivors or victims. So Andrew's front door is wide open. We can walk right in and look for survivors and victims ourselves. I have to tell William to come on. I don't know why he's reluctant. We've left IOUs all over my neighborhood.

It is impossible to see what the order was on the bottom floor of the house. I can tell which room was which because the sofa could not float through an open door, nor could the bed, but nothing else is in its right place. The stench indoors is worse than the decay outdoors. This is death, but it is probably garbage. Outside the sun has cooked everything soupy so it's not this bad. I gag. "Get out of the kitchen," William says, gently taking my arm. I am wearing sandals, and the water in the first level of the house is four inches deep when I can't use books and cushions as stepping stones. "You want to keep going?" William says. "There's something I need to see," I say.

We walk through the house. The second level is different, because the flood water came in but didn't move anything.

Here is their formal living area, where everything is ruined but nothing is moved. I am looking for their treasures. I'm sure Andrew rushed right into shared treasures with Sarah. Things that will last and entangle her even if the mortgage gets paid off, even if she tries to leave him. I see framed photographs. Water has come up and gone down, and even though it has washed the color in the photographs in the frames so that the primary colors are separating around the edges where it seeped, I can figure out who the subjects are at the centers. This is what I want to see. "I don't need to see anything else," I say to William as I go around the room gingerly, examining every picture I can find. A few have fallen; none has been ruined beyond recognition.

There are several photos of Andrew and Sarah together, of course. And photos of young people who resemble her enough that I can figure out that they must be her children. I find a framed photo of Andrew's parents that I remember from our house. They must have been in their fifties when it was taken. His father has a lei around his neck, and his mother is smiling about as broadly as one glass of wine would allow a teetotaler.

I find no more, so I insist we go look in the bedroom. I'm sure it's pointless, but I go anyway. The bedroom is above the flood line, so it is intact, looking like a room anyone would have left hurriedly before a trip. Bed made imperfectly, laundry basket in the middle of the room with clothes that weren't washed in time, jewelry on the dresser that wasn't valuable enough to take along for what should have been three days. The bedside tables have no photographs. Nor do the dressers. In fact, the room has not one sentimental item in it. That is not what matters to me.

"I knew it," I say, out loud. I sit down on the bed, motion for William to sit beside me. He sits a foot away. I pat the space next to myself; he moves closer. I begin taking my clothes off. "What do you notice about the photographs?" I say.

William considers. "I'd say Andrew is a man with no past."

I am in my underwear, and I begin removing his clothes.

"I wonder whether he told her he had children," I say. William shrugs. He's distracted. "I wonder if he quit telling himself he had children." William kisses me, long and deep and silent. I forget where I am, what I am thinking. He slips off my panties, unhooks my bra, doesn't stop kissing me. "Leaving *me* I can forgive," I say softly. "You shouldn't," William says, and then I have no more to say.

NOT MUCH
GOOD AT COMPANY

When Charles took the job in the public library on the east bank of the river in 1976, his mother didn't move. It was the first time since he left for college that she did not follow him, to Baton Rouge and Hammond for five years of school, credits trailing behind him as he tried to escape, to San Francisco when he thought the dirtiness of the young people would put her off, to New York when he got a whiff of anonymity. Resigned, he returned to New Orleans, to their old neighborhood off General DeGaulle Drive on the west side of the river, hoping he would be like the magician who could stiffen a rope and push instead of pull.

She was past sixty by then, eligible for the highrise behind the Winn-Dixie, and the rents were so low, the apartments so airtight, that she chose not to follow him when he moved into New Orleans proper. Charles was willing to concede anything, so they set up their schedule, after work Tuesdays and Thursdays, all day Saturday. She ironed his shirts and saved the Sunday Times-Picayune for him; he drove her to Schwegmann's where the prices were lower than at Winn-Dixie, never mind that the place smelled of fish every day of the week, not just Fridays.

He bought a house for $15,000. Mrs. duQuesnay had lived in that house since her marriage; her late husband was brought there as a newborn when the bargeboard walls that held up the roof still carried the dampness of the river from which they'd been scavenged. Charles felt no particular sorrow when, two years later, Mrs. duQuesnay got word to him that, had she known her hip was going to mend so well, she never would have sold her house and moved in with her daughter. A house for $15,000 was not much of a bargain in 1976, especially when Charles had discovered the hard way that nothing covered the bargeboards but paste-hardened wallpaper and a layer of cotton netting. He tore it off in August, hating the pattern of tiny yellow vines, not believing in cold weather, and by November he was wearing a coat indoors, knowing all the heat was flying up to the high ceiling or out the one-inch cracks between the dark boards. Mrs. duQuesnay had taken advantage of him, but he sensed that she loved the wallpaper and would not want to see the house now, sensed, too, that once she got over the wallpaper, she would offer him less than he paid. When her great-niece two houses down hinted that it would be nice to have Mrs. duQuesnay in for a visit, Charles always said, "I'm not much good at company," but she kept it up until Charles saw Mrs. duQuesnay in the Sunday obits last year and breathed a sigh of relief. By then he had saved up enough to call LAS Enterprises and have dun-colored aluminum siding installed before the Historic District Landmarks Commission could descend on his neighborhood and make up rules for hundred-year-old houses. When the LAS truck drove up, his neighbors took turns standing on the sidewalk and glaring at his house, and Charles was almost glad it was Saturday; watching his mother quibble with herself over Royal versus Jell-O while grocery carts slammed behind her peevishly was a better way to spend the day.

The price on gelatin desserts was the same for both brands, and his mother could not decide. "Read me the box," she said. He told her he didn't have his glasses. "You don't need glasses," she said. "You had 20/20 vision all through school." Reading glasses, he explained. "It's that silly job of yours; why you ruin your eyes for minimum wage is beyond me." Charles watched a yellow-haired woman with two white-haired babies in her cart try to maneuver past his mother. On the west bank, she would have bad teeth and mean vowels, but her panties peeked out from the bottom of her shorts, and that was enough.

"Not minimum wage, Mama," Charles said with no feeling. This was not the time to remind her that any man his age would need reading glasses if he ever used his eyes at all. "Aren't we the grump today," his mother said.

In the elevator in her building, his arm muscles straining from carrying ten plastic grocery bags in a single trip, Charles told his mother about the neighbors.

"I don't know why you live over there, everybody so high and mighty, like living that close to colored people gives them permission to judge anything you do."

Charles laughed, sidled out of the elevator, his saddlebags thumping against the doors. His mother held her door key in both hands, aimed in readiness, at lock level. "Even if you couldn't see daylight through your walls, you have every right to seal off that place. The utility rates over there…"

"Are the same as over here."

His mother let out a little huff of annoyance, and he was sorry he'd ever described his house to her. She never had visited him, in fact had crossed the river only once, on Christmas, when Charles had driven her through the empty downtown streets to the Westin for a dinner that set him back seventy dollars and did not please her particularly.

He stayed until nightfall, listening to her ragings about New Orleans just enough to keep him sure that he did not like her as a person. In New York, she despised the Pakistanis, went out of her way to learn their identifying markers, their

196

names in taxicabs, their wares in train stations. In San Francisco, she liked to career across sidewalks and bruise the shins of gay men with the cart she used to pull home her bags of groceries. "If you don't like it here, you could go somewhere else," he said, as he had said many times in other cities. "Choose a place," she always said back.

"You got a colored mayor; you get a colored city," she was saying.

"You sure it's not the other way around?" Charles said. She frowned at him, as if he'd gone into obscure reaches of logic to annoy her. "You get a colored city; you get a colored mayor." As soon as the words were out, he was sorry. Going back to scurry past his neighbors might be a more dignified way to spend the afternoon.

"So explain New York to me. You got Giuliani; you got a white city back." She folded her arms atop her untethered bosom and smiled.

"Anyway, what I've always liked here is you can tell the bad people from a distance."

***

The woman was sitting on her front steps across the street when he returned. Her feet were planted far apart, her elbows rested on her knees, her chin was mashed down on the heels of her hands, pressing her mouth into a pout. In the dark, the white of her panties between her splayed legs shone as if she had a light in there.

"They say they hope your weatherboards rot," she said from across the street.

Charles shrugged. "And?"

"And you'll never resell it."

"I plan to die here. It's not my problem," he said, then turned and walked inside.

Before he turned on the light, he pulled aside the curtain covering the glass on the door a fraction of an inch. She already was on her way into the house. He realized that she had distracted him so he hadn't looked at the new siding. But that was good: if it had drawn his attention, then it would not serve its purpose, to make the house seem to disappear.

She was there in the morning when he went to look. He would have preferred to shamble out to pick up the newspaper, but he didn't subscribe. He had subscribed when he first came back to New Orleans, but his mother had grilled him on articles she had read, and he had skipped all of them. When she told him that he might as well not read it unless someone else had scanned it for him first, he canceled. He read the *New York Times* at the library on his lunch break, but he never told her. There was no overlap: his mother red-lined stories about fires, freezes, and deaths by multiple gunshot wounds, all in the Metro section. He never asked her whether they were cautionary tales because, oddly, he sensed that she simply enjoyed them.

"It looks real," the woman called. "I can see how they tried to make it like genuine wood grain and all."

"Thanks," he said, assuming that was what she wanted.

She crossed the street toward him as if she'd just thought of doing so. "I'm Audrey," she said.

"Thanks," he said again, and he didn't take the hand she offered.

"You want some coffee or something?" she said.

"I live right here," Charles said.

"I mean, it's Sunday morning, you know, people don't generally have anything to do on a Sunday morning."

Charles had his day slotted into small pockets. For him, Sunday was much like Monday, Wednesday, and Friday: he did not have to cross the river. From nine to five he worked as hard as if he were at the library, wash two loads, wipe the baseboards, wax, dust, Windex. Twenty minutes for lunch, canned soup, hot to fill the time. Weed, mow, edge, prune. She'd been living across the street for a while if he could judge by the dust on the porch. The owner had the front pressure-washed between tenants, a noisy process impossible to ignore. She should have known how he spent his Sundays.

"I'm subletting," she said that afternoon when he came out to clear the amaryllis bed. He disliked amaryllis, but the bulbs had been in the ground when he bought the house and each year popped up red and triumphant. At first he thought he would yank them out when they went to bulb as soon as Mrs. duQuesnay died, but each year they came back fuller, claiming more space, it seemed, making them harder to replace.

"Oh," Charles said, not looking up at Audrey, hoping she'd go away. In the library, lonely people could be driven off easily this way.

She told him she played the bass in the orchestra, that Vlad played bass, too, but he was away on auditions, the orchestra was in such bad straits who wouldn't go off on auditions, but she had a fight with her roommate, and here she was, using Vlad's apartment, who knew what she'd do next?

"I hate cats," Charles said as he removed a trove of feces from beneath the yellow shoots of a newly emerging plant. Audrey tiptoed over to look, as if Charles had found rare antique glass fragments in his flower bed. "With dogs, they're supposed to be on leashes, you have recourse," he said. "Cats, all you can do is call the pound, and they're as likely to have the money to come out as anyone else around here."

Audrey bounced on the balls of her feet, the only part of her visible to Charles if he chose to cast a glance in her direction.

"You know, you can control animals just so much," she said. "I mean, I want my cat inside, but if she runs past me out the door, there's not a whole lot I can do." Charles said nothing, knowing there was plenty she could do, trapping it behind one door before opening another, using the shotgun plan of a house like the airlocks in a submarine. This was not something he needed to learn in the library; this was common sense. "I'm just lucky she doesn't try to go back to my old house," Audrey was saying. "It's on the other side of Magazine Street, and no cat can make it across two-way traffic."

"What's it look like?" Charles said, trying to be polite but asking a question that couldn't take long to answer.

"Why do you want to know?"

"So I can kill it if it comes in my yard," he said, annoyed at her reaction, and she walked away.

"You're a good-looking young man," his mother said when he told her Audrey was watching him.

"I'm fifty-two," he said.

"Well, you don't look it," his mother said, as if this were the first intimation she'd had of his true age.

Charles knew better: he had noticed tiny lines behind his ears, old man lines that came of trim haircuts and hours bent over unshaded gardens. His whiskers were all silver, though Audrey was the only person who'd seen him unshaven in many years, and she had seen him through the myopia of a Sunday morning. If she'd noticed, she hadn't been deterred, instead may have been drawn by a sign that he was old enough to take care of someone else.

"What's the girl do?" his mother said.

"I don't know. I don't even know her name."

"Good." She added more sugar to his coffee. "You already have enough troublesome neighbors. You don't need one more."

He found two symphony tickets in his mailbox that night

when he returned home. A Post-It note attached read, "for you and your friend, Audrey," in green ink, lower case letters so fine and smooth and close together they appeared to be written on rubber stretched vertically. He stood on the porch and waited, and she was on her steps in the time it took him to inhale and exhale once.

"I don't understand," he said.

She cocked her head to the side, and she aged under the street light, shadows on jowls, a thin undercoat of gray in her yellow hair. A child of forty. "Your friend," she said.

He understood. When he worked reference, women would come in with intense interest in hummingbird gardens or lupus, and after a few days they would say, "So how does your wife manage on a librarian's wages?" and he would say, "Oh, her parents are wealthy," and the women would tire of hummingbirds or decide they were not sick after all, and he wouldn't see them again. "I don't have a friend," he said to Audrey.

"Oh, yes, you do," she said. "You go out three nights a week and come back fed."

"How do you know?"

"You only put out your garbage every other Friday," she said, and Charles had to laugh.

"Come on in," he said, now that he was safe.

"Oh, good lordy Jesus," she said when she saw his bargeboard walls. He was used to them; he also assumed that she had peered across the street often enough to have had a

202

glimpse of what lay past his front door, but perhaps from a distance all one saw was an unreadable darkness.

"Bargeboards," he said, and he told her of their origins.

"Calm down," she said, "you're talking like you're reciting the encyclopedia."

He was sorry he'd let her in.

"I wouldn't mind a cup of coffee," she said. He looked at his watch, though he knew the time. "I sleep in the daytime," she said. "Music, you know." Charles wanted to say, Well, I don't sleep in the daytime, but she'd ask him where he worked, and he didn't want her to know. Though she already might have looked him up in the city directory: all the branch libraries had copies. "You have to be at work by nine, right?" she said.

"Good guess."

"You leave at eight-forty. Name one place in New Orleans you can't get to in New Orleans in twenty minutes." She was bouncing on the balls of her feet again—without discernible rhythm.

"Maybe I work across the river."

"Against traffic, ten minutes." She moved closer to him.

"The airport?"

"Traffic coming in there, too. Fifteen minutes." Now she was two feet from him. "You work at the library on Loyola."

"I don't like this," he said, and she stepped back.

"There's something about you," she said. "I suppose you remind me of someone." Her voice was low, but not sensuous enough to frighten him. "I want to touch you," she said then, and he felt numbness, the retraction that begins in the balls when a sight is unbearable, two men kissing, a dog bludgeoned to death, his mother's thigh.

"I don't like to be touched," he said.

She took his hand, ran her fingers across the back of it. Soft, slender fingers, not bass player fingers, he was not aroused, she was not going to excite him, she lifted his hand to her mouth, kissed the palm, and when she moved to kiss his mouth, he came toward her, kissed her angrily until he couldn't stop kissing her. She reached for the front of his pants, felt nothing, only loose fabric, and he pulled away.

"I don't like to be touched," he said again.

She went away quickly, and Charles decided he was on to something.

***

The doorbell rang Sunday morning at seven-forty, and Charles didn't answer, but he tiptoed to the front, planned to crack the door curtain when he heard footsteps leaving the porch. It rang again, he didn't move. Polite knocking on the wooden door frame: he was trapped by someone listening for his footsteps. The heel of a fist on the glass.

"I know you're in there."

A woman's voice, not Audrey's, not his mother's. A white woman's voice, traces of the Irish Channel in the five syllables, not the heartland-to-California anchor voice of his spoiled neighbors. "Charles!" Chawls. He flung open the door as if that had been his intention all along. Mrs. duQuesnay's great-niece, whose name he'd forgotten by 1978.

She stepped into his living room as if she did so every Sunday at seven-forty a.m. "I should of known," she said, looking at the bargeboards. "I should of known."

Charles folded his arms across his chest, waited. He would give her one minute to quit insulting him, and then he would take a step or two toward her, frighten her into leaving. No lights were on in the living room, the shutters were closed; the only illumination came through the pale curtain on the door window. She went for the switch on the far wall with that keenness of memory that retains the lay of a room when all else is gone.

"This time you went too far," she said.

"What."

"Go look," she said.

Charles shrugged his shoulders, and she took his wrist and pulled him toward the door. He pulled away from her.

"You can tell me where to go look."

"As if you need telling." She pointed toward the front, and he opened the door. In the middle of the street was a lake of shattered glass, thick and ice-green, a few shards glinting in the early morning sun. Car window glass. Not his. His car was parked on a small cement apron next to his house. His mother told him in 1976, "You are so close to the St. Thomas those colored boys will steal your car every week if you don't park it under your bedroom window. The last thing you need is to find out some murderer used your car and left blood all over it. The police'd never give it back, you know."

The parking slab was next to his living room, but his mother didn't know that. For a while he'd quit bothering to pull up there when car thieves had broken in anyway, discovered he had manual transmission, splintered his gear shift to get even, left.

Now, though, breaking car windows was a game of skill, one rock, one pitch, high speed, hit the dead center of the glass, and it would break into hundreds of rough-edged pieces, fall to the street. Charles's street ran one-way downtown, a nice target range for St. Thomas Project boys on their way home to get out the last anger of a night; he was sure a pile of glass could be found in each block from Napoleon to Jackson.

"Probably some boys from the project," Charles said.

"Now what's the point of blaming someone else when you're trying to get even?" the great-niece said. "Though that's about what we'd expect."

"If you're blaming me for this, you're sadly mistaken," Charles said, moving between the woman and his door.

"I don't think so. Audrey told everyone what happened."

Charles looked across the street. Audrey's car, the driver's window space reflecting nothing, framing the disarray of her front seat, a jagged rim of glass along the lower perimeter. "What happened," he repeated, sick and curious. He assumed Audrey was watching.

"That poor girl," the woman said, working her way toward the steps and preparing to run. "You don't fit in here, you know."

"I don't want to fit in here," Charles said and walked back into the house before she could get away.

***

He didn't give his mother the story on Tuesday or Thursday, but let it coalesce. She sat in silence as he told her in the car on the way to the grocery, when he had to face forward. "So the neighbor pounds on my door at seven-forty on a Sunday morning, tries to pull me out into the street. Shows me this girl's car, its window shattered. Says she and everyone else knows I did it."

His mother said nothing until they pulled into the parking lot. "Well did you?" she said.

BASKET

He was in the cereal aisle of the Winn-Dixie on Tchoupitoulas Street when he heard the boy, in earnest high treble, say to his mother, "You're not watching the basket, you better watch the basket," and the mother laughed. He supposed mothers were entitled to laugh by mid-summer, having heard too much nonsense, but it rankled nevertheless.

"No one can steal what we haven't paid for," the mother said with a little too much like contempt. All he had was a pound box of brown sugar and a carton of oatmeal in his hands, and he trailed them all the way to the dairy case, deposited the sugar and oatmeal next to the cream cheese, waited until neither the boy nor the mother was paying attention, rolled the basket away as smoothly as if it were his, checked out.

He brought home quite a life that day, and he was as pleased as an anthropologist, piecing together clues. The mother was a woman of resignation; she had given in on chocolate in three places, had sprung for a fishing lure, a weapons magazine.

In the basket, too, was an ironing board cover, tasteful, ticking-striped, and a sympathy card without Bible verse or rhyme. He realized he had moved too soon, for the woman had not reached the produce aisle, and for the $87 he paid at the register he found himself spending the week eating Count Chocula while poring over pages of ads for ultra varmints and feather guardian angels, berettas and glocks, none of which he ever had dreamed could be owned legally. He acceded a certain admiration to the boy's mother; his own had led him to believe that the simple act of touching a gun, even a photograph of one, would lead to certain death.

The ironing board cover pleased him immensely, for he had had an iron and bare metal board for so long that he doubted he had been the one to purchase either, and he long ago had given up on smoothing his clothes, detesting the clang of iron against bare aluminum, the cloth in between taking on the imprint of the pattern of circles on the board. He ironed one shirt, then another, then all that hung in his closet, enjoying his success, enjoying, too, the scent of fabric softener the woman had selected.

By the end of the week only the fishing lure was of no use. Even the card had purpose, though he felt out of line not using it as it was intended. He covered a BB hole in a window with an opalescent calla lily, cut from the front of the card. He scanned his apartment for somewhere to hang the shiny aluminum minnow, tried the pull cord on the ceiling fan, pricked his finger nastily on its hook.

He was thinking about going to a new store, taking a new basket; if he kept this up he was going to have more trophies like the fishing lure. A cork board would be nice for displaying them. The Sav-A-Center on Veterans Boulevard had a complete aisle of stationery supplies. He would wait for someone to buy a cork board, take the basket after the produce aisle. After a week of chocolate, fruit would be a good change, though he knew he had no right to hope that whoever bought a cork board also would buy food.

Stationery supplies were on the aisle with paperback fiction. But after twenty minutes of romance novels, detective stories, lipstick pinks and blood reds, all with covers full of determination, he realized he was going about this all wrong, that the cork board was something exactly right for his use. So he left the stationery aisle. Unattendedness was all he required in a basket. He found one in the produce aisle.

He had taken the basket of someone poor and black with as yet undetected high blood pressure. It was in the meat. Hidden under the canned goods, though he wouldn't have been swayed if he'd seen it before. Slabs of sweet pickle pork, five-pound package of ground beef, chicken wings. Bologna. He never had known a black person well, but he knew what black people put in their baskets in supermarkets. "I'm not saying nothing," the clerk said.

He swam in fat for a week, quit wiping his mouth, felt his body fill up with slow grease. He never felt sick, and he began to enjoy not fearing for his health. His shopper had filled the undershelf of the basket with a case of canned Coke. He was obligated to finish it before he went out again for food, and his head buzzed with pleasure and caffeine. He wondered what he would do if he one day found the undershelf of a basket bearing dog food or cat litter.

His shoppers took care of him, providing light bulbs and toilet paper just when he thought he never was going to find them. Autumn impulses of others warmed him, with cider and cocoa and fat squashes. He felt he did not cheat at Thanksgiving, went past the meat aisle before he took a basket, willing to bake a turkey if one came along. But he had timed his trip to the store for Wednesday, so for Thanksgiving he had had only last-minute foods, a fresh pie, mint pillows, parsley, raw cranberries.

He got caught the week before Christmas at Delchamps. The basket was parked in front of the American cheeses, and no one was on the aisle except a woman wiggling jumbo eggs to check for cracks. We walked past her, commandeered the basket, kept moving.

"Hey," she called out after him, an open carton of eggs

211

still in her hand. She was as broad as she was tall, as one might have expected on that aisle, but she moved at a good clip, eggs riding smoothly. He looked down at what she had selected so far, working on explanations, but the basket was full of items no self-respecting man would buy, foolish decorations, a plastic Santa and reindeer that would light up with a twenty-five-watt bulb inside, ornaments of elves looking ridiculously happy, a string of tiny pink tree lights. She also had four pies.

"My mind must have been a million miles away," he said, trying to pull her into the spirit of the season, but she would have none of it.

"I don't think so," she said, and she pushed her basket away with greater speed than he would have thought possible. "I spent half an hour picking out those decorations," she called back to him. You should have spent another half hour, he thought to himself, relieved. He left the store with nothing.

For a few weeks after Christmas, he felt mopey and ascetic, and he took no baskets. He wasn't as sure of his future as he had been before he was caught, but he was willing to wait as long for himself as he was for others. Until he regained his direction, he would stay out of supermarkets, go European, feel French and existentialist, which was a way of feeling nothing at all; if he wanted bread he went to the Sunbeam outlet, for fruit he went to the green truck, for chicken to Popeyes; nothing would last more than a day. He wished he could remember the time before ice boxes, when everything and nothing was fresh, when, his mother had told him, you could get banty eggs, warm by the side of the road, eat them without a moment of cooling.

The white of bread, the brown of meat, the green of vegetables: he was going out to obey rules, of balanced plates; the rest was up to him. He could not possibly know if the rules were right for him. Perhaps he was supposed to be a person who needed an overload of certain enzymes or acids; perhaps he was a person who would achieve perfect tranquility in a roomful of pink lights. For three days he did not go out, figuring that soon his body would ache for what he needed. He had read of women who ate clay, of children who chose turnip greens in cafeteria lines. When he woke one morning hoping he would want nothing but chocolate, he decided he needed chocolate.

His check came in the noon mail. He went to the Rite-Aid drugstore, took a carry basket. At the bottom he placed solid bars of chocolate, then he began to crave other textures, and he added Toblerone bars, Almond Joys, Snickers, Nestle's Crunch. Nuts and crisps: he might go on from here next time. He would have to see.

THE HOLY ASSUMPTION OF MR. TINSEL

People often passed as Walter let himself in through the street door, but no one ever turned to look. It seemed to him that having keys to a door on Bourbon Street counted for something, but even down at his end everyone was looking for women and men in feathers and spangles, and he never attracted any curiosity, any particular envy.

He didn't like having to go through the narrow corridor to the stairs, and he'd have liked some admiration for doing so every day. He'd once figured that the passage was half a block long, and so high, two stories up to the ceiling, that if there was a light fixture at all, it hadn't had a bulb in it for as long as he could remember. A queer little slit of a transom was set over the door at the street, thick and semi-opaque with the grease and dust thrown off by bad behavior.

By late fall no light filtered through, and now, with the winter solstice only a few weeks away, all Walter could do was leave the street door open, open maybe to prying eyes of tourists and desperate project boys, while he checked to see that all was the same as ever, and then he'd slam the door, count ninety-seven paces, careful to keep on a straight line so that his white shirt, still clean, would sweep no slick wet walls, take no mildew. Too, he'd given himself quite a nick in the shoulder once, bumping into the row of electric meters which he now knew were on the wall eighteen paces in. Ninety-six steps, and then his hand would find the banister in the dark.

For the past few weeks, Walter had been having a strange experience every time he was walking down the corridor. He tried not to let the thoughts let their way into his mind, but still the image of Riley popped into his head, there in the dark. Riley hadn't lived there in twenty-one years, but lately something about being in the hallway made him think about the man who'd lived in the apartment that shared a landing with his before Dorcas moved in.

Riley was fat. And Riley lived with his father, who was fat, too. The two of them never left their apartment at the same time, and rarely left it at all, but a few times Walter had found himself coming in or going out at the same time as Riley. He could hear Riley puffing slowly through the corridor, too large to move straight forward, sidling along; when Riley reached the electric meters he had to line himself up perpendicularly to the outside door, grunting from little scrapes and bruises. When they came to light, Riley smiled at Walter, and Walter felt he was a friend of sorts.

Riley's father died one morning. Through a crack in his apartment door, Walter could see the police arrive. They went for what seemed like a very short time, reeled out as if they'd seen or smelled something overpowering, one heading back down the steps, flashlight in hand, the other calling after him, "Hey look out for stalactites." "Stalagmites," the first one called back. "How you gonna tell which way's up in a place like this?" said the one still upstairs, and Walter heard a deep hoot of derision come from the corridor below.

It took the ambulance attendants almost two hours to arrive, and Riley stood in his doorway all that time, with Walter watching politely. The attendants had a terrible time getting Riley's father out to the street, their stretcher bearing a great mound, covered in taut rubber.

"This sonofabitch gonna need twenty pallbearers," one said, grunting the way a person does when something won't go around a corner, no matter what. Riley walked slowly behind them, a slow-motion processional; his eyes were red-rimmed now, darting a little, expecting something.

Riley left the door to his apartment wide open. Walter wanted very much to see how they managed to get through the downstairs passageway, but he couldn't think of a discreet way to follow them down the old wooden steps to listen. When Riley didn't return in about four weeks, Walter slipped into his apartment and took the vinyl reclining lounger. He was glad he did it, because a couple of days later the landlord put all of Riley's stuff out on the sidewalk.

Dorcas moved in shortly after that, and she'd lived there ever since. She was a night nurse with about seventeen cats, and Walter could never figure out how she always looked so crisp when she lived with all those cats. She baked him a cake once, courteously leaving it outside his doorway while he was at work, and he'd brought it to the store the next day. He put it on the lunchroom table at noon, cutting a big swath out of it to show he wasn't afraid of cat hairs, but no one else took any all the time he was in the lunchroom. He figured that one of the bus girls took it home, because it was gone when he came in for lunch the next day.

Walter was basically happy with the experiences he'd had with his neighbors, and he thought his place was supreme. He felt that over the years he had made his one-room apartment into a real bachelor pad. He had a refrigerator, a bed with wooden headboard and footboard, a dresser, and a black-and-white console television that his aunt Pearl had left him, and of course the recliner. The bed stood next to the wall, making it a little hard to make up each morning, but he felt it was worth the trouble. He'd won a painting at the store's Fourth of July picnic eight years ago, and the painting was as long as the bed, so it looked perfect hanging on that wall. It was quite a piece of art, a locomotive coming from the valley up the steep rise of a mountainside, as perfect as a photograph.

Walter's refrigerator always had a few beers in it, along with a paper sack in which a half-eaten doughnut had sat for about eight months. At first he'd planned to eat the rest of the doughnut, then he'd considered throwing it away, and with the lapse of time he'd eventually become unable even to peer into the sack, which was neatly folded closed at the top.

Walter liked the image of himself when he was home. He'd take a beer out of the refrigerator, turn on Channel Six, the only channel poor Aunt Pearl's TV could pick up anymore, and plop himself down in his recliner. He was sure he looked exactly like those guys he saw on TV who sat in front of their own sets, throwing back beers, jumping up and down excitedly while a crowd roared on the tube, and trying to ignore their nagging wives who were always harping about some kind of dish detergent. Walter was an all-American man. Once or twice it occurred to him that it was too bad that Aunt Pearl and Riley's father had had to die before he got the television and the recliner. He might have invited Riley over to watch a football game.

He was lucky that, if his TV could only pick up one channel, it would be Channel Six. Walter had his own television show; at least five weeks out of the year he did. He was the creator of Mr. Tinsel, whom he tended and succored and curried forty-seven weeks out of the year. Every weeknight from mid-November to Christmas Eve, Mr. Tinsel was on TV at five forty-five. For the past couple of years, Walter had been bothered that Mr. Tinsel was followed by the Muppets. He didn't know why exactly, but the Muppets made him feel bad. The toy department was full of books and stuffed dolls and games with Muppet pictures on them, and the only Mr. Tinsel for kids was an inflatable balloon toy that Newman's brought out every Christmas for a dollar sixty-nine. The colors on it weren't even close to correct. He once asked George, who was a producer at Channel Six, why the Muppets followed his show.

"You come on first; that way the kids keep watching," George said. Walter liked George after that, but he still didn't particularly care for the Muppets.

He'd taped today's episode only yesterday morning, and it was fresh enough in his mind to keep him chuckling with anticipatory laughter. That Mr. Tinsel was a feisty one; it was hard to remember sometimes that he was a marionette. Walter had fashioned the original Mr. Tinsel out of lamp globes and chandelier bulbs—some as delicate as eggshells and painted with iridescent paint—and Christmas tree tinsel twenty years ago. Mr. Tinsel was supposed to look as if he were made of Christmas tree ornaments, and the general manager of Newman's department store had been delighted with the idea of using the fragile puppet to promote Christmas toy sales. Over the years, Mr. Tinsel became a media celebrity and in the process eventually had had every globe shattered and replaced. Walter had put him through several metamorphoses, and these days he was made of kapok sheathed in shiny Mylar. These days, too, Walter didn't have to do live television, so he could go home and watch the taped broadcast of the program in the comfort of his own recliner.

In today's episode, Mr. Tinsel was trying to educate his thickheaded moose friend, Choklit, about barber poles and magnetic poles. Their painted-on eyes swayed in and out of focus as marionette eyes do, though Walter had tried to aim them as much as possible toward a red-and-white barber pole standing like a monolith on the puppet stage. Mr. Tinsel and Choklit were caught up in an absolutely uproarious conversation. "I think I've, uh, found the, uh, North Pole here, Mr. Tinsel. Uh, looks like a, uh, candy cane. Except, you know, uh, there's no hook." Simple people said "uh" a lot. Choklit's cloven hand made a smooth arc in the air, and Walter shimmered with the pleasure that comes of pure talent.

Walter knew that in all their homes, all over the city, little Santa-believing kids were squealing, "No, silly, that's not the North Pole!" So that's exactly what Mr. Tinsel said, "No, silly, that's not the North Pole!" in a voice that was the same one Walter used in his everyday life. Mr. Tinsel was goodhearted, and he always stood out as the leader among all the characters. Walter saw him as a wellspring of information, though it wasn't easy to gauge how much the children were learning from his shows. Walter never had talked to children, though he eavesdropped on them whenever he was near them in the store.

Each plot also had to give Walter a lead to talk about toys that Santa would bring and about how the kids who were friends of Mr. Tinsel's should come down to see Santa and all his toys at Newman's. Mr. Tinsel was good for Newman's department store.

In fact, Mr. Tinsel was so good for the store that tomorrow a three-story-tall model of the puppet would be mounted on the façade of the building, which had dominated Canal Street since 1903. Newman's did that every year, so kids whose mamas took them down to Canal Street would pester until they got to go to Newman's. The mamas used to be refined white ladies who parked at Solari's; now more of them were black girls who came on the bus with their babies, but every child on earth was horribly spoiled, as far as Walter could tell from the fussing. Newman's had a suburban store now, too, but Walter never had seen it, and he couldn't see that it mattered much. Walter couldn't wait until tomorrow, when a hollow plaster-case Mr. Tinsel would have his holy assumption over Canal Street.

His thoughts were broken by the deep-falsetto voice of Kermit the Frog, and Walter knew he was finished with television for the evening. He tipped the recliner slightly forward, until his toe could reach the on-off button on the TV. Once the old set had swallowed the picture into the center of itself, Walter swiveled around until he could reach the refrigerator. He prided himself on being able to control his whole world from a sitting position, and he pulled a second beer from the meat compartment right under the little freezer of his refrigerator. He liked his beer icy cold.

Walter liked to think he was a valued employee of Newman's because he wasn't a ten-to-six person; he lived his job. During his days he wrote scripts and refurbished his puppets and, at Christmas season, he taped a show each weekday. But, really, he'd given up his nights to his job, too, because he was a creative person, and his mind had to be working all the time. Tonight, he decided, he would have to start working up plots in which Mr. Tinsel could be more hero-like; kids were crazy about that kind of thing, if he could judge by what he saw on the shelves of the toy department. He wouldn't have weapons, of course, the way so many of the good warriors did; he would have a cape and a reassuring voice, and that would be enough.

Mr. Tinsel deserved a chance to show how he could save lives and have girls falling in love with him; that was logical for a fellow who knew all the answers to all the questions. Perhaps he'd begin by creating Mrs. Tinsel — wait, no, that might make Mr. Tinsel look as if he were nothing more than part of some ornamental species. Walter wanted him to be one of a kind. Well, Walter thought, tipping back the cold beer in the dry-heated room, I have to figure out how to introduce someone for Mr. Tinsel to rescue. She should have about as much savvy as those girls the store hired every year straight out of high school to work in the hosiery department, he planned. As light and delicate as air. With no kapok. And a great deal of gratitude. Walter was well on his way to next year's series when he fell asleep at seven-thirty.

Usually he could manage to be on his way to work by first light, because he always fell asleep so early. This particular morning, though, he was already perched on a counter stool at Chez Donut while the sky was still matte black. Walter wasn't tamping down his excitement at all, clacking thick china cup against saucer with the idea that a thirty-six-foot Mr. Tinsel was going to defy all the laws of gravity that ruled Canal Street.

Even after he had drunk two cups of hot chocolate, the doughnut seemed too dry to swallow, and when the clock behind the cash register reached seven o'clock, Walter decided he'd had enough to do with breakfast. Ever the one to profit from experience, he left the bitten-out doughnut on the plate.

Chez Donut was on Iberville Street, the first street that ran parallel to Canal inside the French Quarter; it was one-way toward the river, lined with the rude, flat backsides of stores.

Walter couldn't actually see the façade of Newman's until he rounded the corner onto Canal. When he turned, the little streaks of light in the sky were enough now for him to see a splendid sight: there lay Mr. Tinsel, a good part of a city block

223

in length, filling two lanes of the downtown side of a street that soon would be busy with buses, secretaries, shoppers, and hundreds of lost automobiles, their drivers speeding with annoyance. No one ever drove on Canal Street on purpose. Mr. Tinsel was protected only by a cadre of orange traffic cones, straight and military watchmen around his Gulliver-body.

Walter figured that the warehousemen must have brought him out late last night. Going by what had been done in years past, Walter knew workmen would begin hoisting Mr. Tinsel up onto the front of the building around nine-thirty, when rush hour was pretty well past and the store still wasn't open for business. It made a lot of sense to Walter.

Walter strolled happily around to the back entrance and let himself into the store with his own key. Only he and the security guard were there this early in the morning, but he treasured padding through the gray silence at an hour when everyone else from the store was still home asleep. One morning he'd worn his church shoes to work, just to be different, and the sound of the hard leather on the polished floors had felt like such a violation of the rules that he'd never worn anything but Hush Puppies slip-ons after that.

Mr. Tinsel and the whole cast of supporting characters were waiting for him in the studio. Walter was never grudging about sharing the spotlight with any of them. As he walked in and flooded the room with fluorescent light, his expression changed, from pure reverence for the dark to beatific pleasure over their sweet patience. "Good morning, guys," he said, and probably his voice could be heard all over the second floor. "Catch that game on TV last night?" Walter's off-stage imaginings about Mr. Tinsel were quite different from the ones he actually could put into scripts. He couldn't have Mr. Tinsel and his friends sitting in front of the television set betting on a football game. "So who do you think's gonna make the playoffs?"

Choklit had been particularly irrepressible lately. Walter moved closer to him, perfectly naturally, and Choklit said, "How about them Mets?" Walter moved along, passing each puppet on the shelf, going through a medley of knowing chuckles. When he reached Mr. Tinsel, Mr. Tinsel said in a kind, tolerant voice, "Oh, they play baseball, you must have your mind on baseball."

"I was just kidding," Choklit said from the corner of Walter's mouth.

Walter gave him a hearty laugh, then clapped his hands once, loudly, wanting the mood to lift. "What a caution," he said. "Now, look, guys, today's a big day, you know." Locker room time; he almost could smell the ammonia. "Your leader will be enshrined on the front of our building." He said "enshrined" as if he just had learned the word. "Now this occasion's gotten me to do a lot of thinking. You're going to see some changes around here! What you fellows need are some women." They all were fully androgynous to an outsider, but Walter never had questioned that the puppets

225

all were men of their species. He marched up and down like a general, knees unbending, strides long. The marionettes sat up neat and straight, their strings hung taut from the shelf above. Walter liked to leave them that way at night, as if they were a team before a game, waiting for him to come in the next morning and give them a talk.

"Okay!" Walter said, and gave another rousing clap, though he wasn't looking into the paint-eyes anymore. He began fingering a chunk of Styrofoam that he'd left on his work table. By Christmas next year Mr. Tinsel would have himself an ingénue.

Nine-thirty passed, ten o'clock arrived, customers began drifting up to the second floor, with the nervous hum of people who are considering spending money, and yet no one had come to tell Walter that it was time to come down to the street to see the sculpture raised onto the store's front. Walter decided at ten-thirty to go out onto Canal Street to check things out, see if he could help. Mr. Tinsel was still where he'd been at daybreak, supine in the middle of the street, guarded by traffic cones. Walter didn't want to approach anyone to find out what was going on, but he moved as close as he could to a crowd of workmen who looked particularly cranky.

"Goddamn," one said. "I like to get killed by that fucking rock. Wouldn't you figure they could of known earlier that this dumb tinker toy can't hang on no building without pulling the whole damn thing down."

"I hate doing shit that's stupid," said another. "Don't tell me it's not fucking stupid, leaving this big bastard in the middle of the street until they fix the building. Old as that building is, we going to be walking over this thing come Easter." He waved his hand over Mr. Tinsel in disgust.

Walter couldn't move. He was more frightened by the men than hurt by their insults, and he didn't take a step away from where he stood until the workmen drifted away, bored and embarrassed. Slowly Walter began a tour around the body. He was looking for cracks, chinks, but Mr. Tinsel seemed perfect, unmoved. Feeling relief that probably Mr. Tinsel actually hadn't been raised onto the building yet, but rather that something had happened when they were attaching the supports, he stepped back just the tiniest bit. A car with Texas plates came tearing past, horn blaring, coming so close that road dust wiped onto Walter's white shirt. "Asshole!" the driver said from his open window. "Close call," Walter said to no one in particular.

Satisfied that everything was under control, that in fact people at his level had no need to be out on the street, Walter headed for the lunchroom.

All store employees except the general manager ate in the single lunchroom, unless, of course, they had the money and the nerve to go out somewhere else and get a meal down in thirty minutes. Walter loved the lunchroom, with its smells of bay leaf and hot peas and women's cologne, and he always took his only meal of the day there.

There were three long rows of tables pushed end to end. Walter always sat down by himself, but he always had someone sitting close by, if not right next to him. He especially liked it when salesgirls clustered near him, chattering about empty, heavenly things. "I swear, my whole paycheck goes on clothes before I even get it. I got to steer clear of Lingerie; you can blow a hundred dollars on stuff nobody sees. Well, almost nobody." Giggles and knowing sniffs. "You look good in yellow, you know it? Me, I wear yellow, I look like I got a disease." They never realized he was there, eating mutely and staring straight at the food on his tray while he listened to them. He marveled to himself that humans could exchange the kinds of information these girls did.

Times came each day, five minutes before the hour or twenty-five minutes after the hour, when almost everyone but Walter filed out of the lunchroom to do some last-minute toileting. Because Walter put in such long hours, no one kept him to a thirty-minute lunch break, and everyone up to the general manager respected that.

Between lunch shifts, the lunchroom was almost quiet, and Walter could hear the piped-in music. He really didn't mind it, because Newman's kept the radio on a pop station, and Walter listened to it to keep up on what was happening in the world. The Craig Marshall show always overlapped with some part of Walter's lunch break, and the sonorous voice, which moved at an unbelievably fast clip, came right

228

out at Walter from the speaker on the wall by the kitchen door.

"Okay! It's a sad time for the rug rats today," Craig said. "What the hell a rug rat is?" one bus girl said to another. "You kids, fool. What else you think squirm around on the rug?"

"In my house plenty," the first one said, and both laughed.

Walter strained to hear over them. "We've had a confirmed report that the holiday hero of all the short people is dead as a doornail. Yes, Mr. Tinsel — " Craig boomed the name the way the voice-over on TV might say Superman or Mighty Mouse after a great buildup. "Mr. Tinsel has gone to his reward, all over the downtown side of Canal Street." He chuckled a little, and Walter was beginning to be confused. "Hey, we've actually been getting calls from moms saying the kids are positively grief-stricken over the passing of their good friend. We'll have more details when Kerry does the news at twenty past and twenty of the hour."

Craig ran the first few measures of a tinny recording of "The Stars and Stripes Forever," and before he'd even cut it off for a full-gut laugh, Walter was out of the lunchroom. He left his dirty dishes on his tray on the table for the first time in all the years he'd worked for Newman's. Walter prided himself on always bringing his tray back to the kitchen.

He didn't stop running until he reached the radio station five blocks from Newman's. It was a tiny cinder block building, a minor landmark only for having been the first

229

radio station in the city. Walter had no trouble walking in, or even finding Craig's studio. Through the glass he could see Craig's mobile mouth moving in quick patter. Craig couldn't see him and dropped a few words when, without warning, Walter pushed his way through the studio door.

"Hey, what you doing?" Craig said, still on the air. It was the same voice Walter had heard in the lunchroom. But Craig didn't look as slick and trim as his male-model voice. He had cowlicks in his hair and acne pits on his cheeks, and he was so fat that he filled his swivel chair, with a thick strip of thigh hanging over the side.

"I'd like to speak on the radio," Walter said shyly. Radio listeners at home and in their cars couldn't hear him, but Walter didn't know that.

A thick-necked engineer, as big as Craig, had picked up on the interruption in the show and had come running to back Craig up. When he saw Walter, whose belt was on the fifth hole, he stopped short, as if Walter were a cockroach he could take his time with.

"Okay, buddy, come along. You want to be on the radio, okay. You get yourself an FCC license, how about it?"

The engineer was edging Walter inch by inch toward the door, and Walter saw his chance to speak rapidly disappearing. Blindly he began struggling and scratching his way out of the man's gentle grip, then grabbed the microphone from in front of Craig.

"Hello, boys and girls," he said. His heart was light. His voice was his regular voice, the one he also reserved for Mr. Tinsel. "I was busy working down at Newman's, and I heard the most awful thing on the radio. Somebody thought I was dead. No, sirree, they must have gotten the wrong fellow. See, I had to lie down on Canal Street until the building got strong enough for me. I'm a big guy, you know, I..."

Craig and the engineer, as thick and gamy as two slabs of meat, had their wits back now, and they managed to pull Walter in one direction and the microphone in another. As the engineer began trying to drag him from the studio, and while Craig tried to move himself back in under him, Walter strained back. Stretching his neck as far as he could and still be able to talk, Walter kept up his speech.

"No, kids, I'm not even sick or hurt."

A sob fought its way out of him against his will.

"I am not dead!" he said before the engineer dragged him away.

Reprinted with permission from *Christmas Stories from Louisiana*